SCREAMERS

JOEL A. SUTHERLAND

D1247608

Scholastic Canada Ltd.

Toronto New York London Auckland Sydney
Mexico City New Delhi Hong Kong Buenos Aires

For Colleen, who kept me laughing through one of the oddest years of my life.

Scholastic Canada Ltd.
604 King Street West, Toronto, Ontario M5V 1E1, Canada

Scholastic Inc.
557 Broadway, New York, NY 10012, USA

Scholastic Australia Pty Limited
PO Box 579, Gosford, NSW 2250, Australia

Scholastic New Zealand Limited
Private Bag 94407, Botany, Manukau 2163, New Zealand

Scholastic Children's Books
Euston House, 24 Eversholt Street, London NW1 1DB, UK

www.scholastic.ca

Library and Archives Canada Cataloguing in Publication

Title: Screamers / Joel A. Sutherland.
Names: Sutherland, Joel A., 1980- author.
Identifiers: Canadiana 2021009365X | ISBN 9781443182782 (softcover)
Classification: LCC PS8637.U845 S37 2021 | DDC jC813/.6—dc23

Cover credits: Cover photos © Antracit/Shutterstock; Yakov Oskanov/Shutterstock; ZargonDesign/Getty Images.
Interior illustration by Maria Nguyen.

6 5 4 3 2 1   Printed in Canada 114   21 22 23 24 25

MIX
Paper from
responsible sources
FSC   **FSC® C016245**
www.fsc.org

CHAPTER
One

"**L**et me go!" Sai said, straining against the bonds that held him to the battered metal chair he sat in. "Let me go right now!"

He was in the anger phase of being held hostage. The adrenalin coursing through his veins was no doubt giving him a boost of strength, but I wasn't concerned he'd be able to break free. After I'd dragged him to the circus tent, I'd tied him up myself, and I'd double-checked and triple-checked that the knots were as tight as possible. The long, thin balloons — the type used to make dogs and swords and crowns at children's birthday parties — dug into Sai's wrists and ankles, pinning him to his chair. I'd used an entire package of balloons to secure each limb. Sai wasn't going anywhere.

Not until I was done with him.

And then he'd be done with this world.

"But we're having such a grand time," I said, walking slowly around to the back of his chair. "And the best is yet to come." I gave my red rubber clown nose a squeeze and it honked loudly in the quiet of the darkened tent, a joyous sound that made Sai whimper pathetically.

He made a last-ditch effort to break his arms free but to no avail. He sighed and sat still, his head slumped forward. After a moment of silence, he said, "Listen, it's not too late. You can let me go. You haven't done anything bad to me yet. I won't tell anyone about any of this — not my friends, not my parents, not the cops. No one! I promise, just . . . let me go. Please."

"Ah yes. The begging stage," I said. "'Please, please, please, let me go. I won't tell, I promise. I'll give you anything you want. I'll sell out everyone close to me. I'll sell my own soul. Just let me go and we'll forget all about this.' Everyone always gets to this stage sooner or later, and everyone always offers the same empty promises. Lies, of course. Like you'd just go back to your normal life after all of this. Like everything would be A-okay, peachy-keen, and you wouldn't spend the rest of your miserable life looking over your shoulder, afraid you'll see my face . . ." I leaned in close to Sai, forcing him to stare at my white face paint, red nose, red lips and thin vertical lines running over my eyes. ". . . staring back at you from the shadows."

With a smile I placed my hands on Sai's shoulders and squeezed — not too hard, just enough for him to feel it. He shivered and tensed.

2

"You're not even real," he said. "You can't be."

"Unfortunately for you, my friend, I'm very, very real." I gave his shoulders another squeeze to prove my point.

"But you, you, you," he said, tripping over his words and sputtering. "You died years ago!"

I walked around to the back of the chair and laughed, a maniacal sound that twisted and crackled and echoed as if my laughter had taken on a life of its own, carrying on long after I'd stopped and bounding throughout the tent. "I see you've reached the disbelief stage," I said. "Can't say I blame you. This must be hard for someone like you to understand, but death didn't stop me." I stepped back in front of Sai. "I still have so many smiles to share!" I smiled wide and felt my painted lips stretch and crack, then chomped my teeth together three times. *Click-click-click!*

A round, quivering tear clung to Sai's eyelashes for a moment before breaking free and running down his cheek.

"Is that a real tear?" I said, genuinely impressed. So impressed that I broke character and dropped my evil-clown voice to speak with my regular voice.

Sai nodded.

"You can cry on command?"

Sai smiled and laughed, then wiped the crocodile tear away. "Yes, I can cry on command, Zoë." He no longer saw the character I'd been pretending to be for our scene, but instead saw the real me: Zoë Winter, star of the hit show

3

Screamers, currently wearing a clown suit and makeup courtesy of the costume and makeup departments.

"Holy cow, Sai!" I said. "I know plenty of professional actors who have starred in a dozen blockbusters and can't even make their eyes get a little wet on their own."

The circus tent — an image only I could see, which had been conjured up by my imagination so I could get into character fully — was replaced by the production office we were in as I returned to reality. I turned to face Clarice and Anthony, who were seated at a table on the other side of the room. Their table was covered in notes, actors' head-shots and coffee cups, and there was a camera on a tripod between them recording everything so we could review the footage later. But I had a feeling we wouldn't need to review Sai's performance. In my mind, he was already a shoo-in.

"It's not easy to just turn on the waterworks like that," I told Clarice and Anthony. "This guy's good." I turned and saw Sai's smile grow even wider.

"I agree with Zoë," Clarice said. "Great performance, Sai." Clarice was a member of the *Screamers* writing team and a frequent director. She turned to face Anthony, the show's producer. "What do you think, Tony?"

"What do I think?" Anthony said. He was nearly eighty years old but still worked just as hard, if not harder, than anyone else on the *Screamers* crew. The show was his baby, which he was fond of reminding us, and he was incredibly protective of it. He was also short on praise and almost impossible to read. When he told you he thought you'd done a good job, you knew you'd done a *great* job. "Well, this is the first screen test of the day during which I haven't checked my phone, not even once."

I turned back to Sai and gave him a concealed thumbs-up.

"All right. Well," Clarice said, stopping the camera, "thanks for coming in, Sai. We'll be in touch."

"Great!" he said enthusiastically. "Thanks again for the opportunity. Acting in an episode of *Screamers* would be a dream come true."

Clarice smiled, and Anthony finally checked his phone. I took a long drink of water, quenching the deep thirst that always followed acting in a tense scene, even if it was only a screen test.

Sai didn't stand to leave.

"Um, can someone untie me?" he asked.

"Oh! Right!" I hastily put down my glass and untied the balloons that held him to the chair. "Sorry about that."

"No need to apologize, Zoë," he said.

After some final courtesies, Sai left the room. Through the slightly open door I could hear his mom ask him how it had gone. He said it had gone really well, and then added, "For a celebrity, Zoë Winter seems really nice. Down to earth. Like a normal kid."

A warm, happy feeling bloomed in my chest and spread through my entire body. *Really nice. Down to earth. Like a normal kid.*

That's all I wanted to be, a normal fourteen-year-old kid, but that's not how most people thought of me. Most people saw what the media wanted them to see — the child star of a hit show, a kid with more money than many would see in their lifetime, a celebrity who only lived on set or the red carpet. Or they saw what they assumed someone like me must be like — a spoiled rich kid who had the world handed to her on a silver platter, all thanks in large part to her unique ability to scream at an unhuman decibel level.

People rarely saw the real me. I was just a kid who liked to act and got a big break a couple of years ago; who was home-schooled by her mom to accommodate the show's production schedule; who couldn't go out in public without some form of disguise; and who was considering quitting, walking away from it all.

Down to earth. That was music to my ears. If Sai got one of the three roles we were casting as part of a nationwide contest, then maybe we'd be, well . . . friends. Hopefully I'd be friends with all of the contest winners.

Don't get ahead of yourself, Zoë, I thought. *You don't want to scare anyone off by being weird or needy.*

"I like him," I told Clarice and Anthony. "Who's next?"

CHAPTER
TWO

The contest had been a huge hit.

It was a marketing campaign to mark the show's fiftieth episode and the season three premiere. Nearly ten thousand kids my age from across the country entered the contest. The production team combed through hundreds of hours of video submissions before inviting ten "regular" kids to the studio in Toronto for a screen test with me to make sure we had what Clarice and Anthony called "chemistry."

After meeting Sai and a couple of kids who were pretty good, we met Aaliyah. She walked into the room and immediately commanded my attention. She marched straight up to me and shook my hand so firmly that I had to admire her confidence. She struck me as more of a star than I was.

"It is so nice to meet you, Zoë," she said. "I'm a big fan of your work."

"Thank you," I said. "It's nice to meet you too."

"Do you think, that is, if it's not too much trouble, we could take a picture before I leave?"

"Maybe," I said noncommittally. With a little luck she'd forget about the picture by the end of the screen test. I tried to stay out of the public eye as much as possible.

She smiled politely and I indicated the chair across the table from Clarice, Anthony and me. We all took our seats.

"Please tell us a little bit about yourself, Aaliyah," Clarice said. "Why did you enter this contest?"

"Well, I'm not only a fan of Zoë's, but I'm a big fan of *Screamers* too. I've watched every episode at least three times, and I've read all the books. I love horror. Shows like *Screamers* have helped me get through some dark times. If I can be brave enough to face my fears while reading or watching a ghost story, I can be brave enough to face my fears in my day-to-day life."

Clarice smiled and Anthony even nodded, which I took to mean he was impressed. But something about what Aaliyah had said gave me a hint of déjà vu.

"All right," Clarice said, looking from Aaliyah to me. "Let's see how you two do together."

I took a moment to tie Aaliyah to the chair with balloons like the ones I'd used for Sai and the others. Clarice had suggested it might be fun during the auditions if I played the part of Beauregard, an evil ghost clown and the villain of the episode, titled "The Scream Queen," that we were

8

preparing for. I'd leapt at the opportunity and had sunk my teeth into the role. In the show I always played the good guy, and I thought it would be fun to play the bad guy for a change . . . even if only during the screen tests.

By the end of filming the second season, I was beginning to feel restless, even a little bored. I was ready for something new, something that challenged me creatively. Not that I would tell anyone that — not even my mom. In the entertainment industry you are only as hot as your last project, and the popularity of *Screamers* showed no signs of slowing down. How could I walk away from that, even if my heart was no longer totally in it? Each episode followed a new group of kids dealing with all kinds of paranormal activity in different parts of the country, so the other stars of the show and I played different characters every week. But my characters were all variations of the same stereotype: the clueless kid who stumbles upon some haunted location and then discovers she's smart and brave enough to save the day. Hooray, yippee, woo-hoo, roll end credits.

Not only was the work already beginning to feel a little repetitive, but I was beginning to feel like I was missing out — missing out on having normal friends, going to a normal school, having a normal childhood. I couldn't even go to the convenience store to buy a chocolate bar without being noticed.

"That was the thrill of a lifetime," Aaliyah said as soon

as we'd finished the scene. "My followers — *friends* — are going to be so jealous that I got to act with you, Zoë."

I shook my head with a smile. "It's no big deal. You were great."

She placed her hand over her heart. "Really? You mean that? Thank you!" She held up her phone with a hopeful look on her face. "Think we can take that picture?"

"Oh, right," I said. "Do you mind if I take a rain check?" I waved a hand in front of my face, indicating my clown makeup. "I don't exactly look my best."

Aaliyah laughed. "You look great, but I get it. Hopefully we'll meet again and I'll get another chance."

Once she'd left, Clarice and Anthony agreed that they both thought she had potential.

"If nothing else, she's enthusiastic," Anthony said. High praise from him.

"And what she said about horror stories making her feel brave enough to face her real-life fears?" Clarice said with an enthusiastic head nod. "Powerful stuff."

That was it! That's what had given me déjà vu. "Yeah, she's a contender," I said. Because she was. Compared to the other girls we had tested for the role, Aaliyah had been the best so far.

But what she'd said about fear was nearly a word-for-word copy of an answer I'd given during a morning-show interview a year or so ago. I hadn't recalled that right away because I have given hundreds, if not thousands, of interviews over the years, many of them scheduled back to back over the course of a single day during press junkets that turned my brain to mush. Had what Aaliyah said been a coincidence? Or had she seen my interview on YouTube and memorized it in the hopes that it would impress us?

Or — scarier thought — was she some sort of stalker? She'd also mentioned multiple times how big of a fan she is, and how cool it was to meet me . . .

I shook my head. No. That was just my imagination running away. She wasn't a stalker.

Probably.

"Have you changed your mind about Aaliyah, Zoë?" Clarice asked. She must have noticed me shaking my head and thought that meant I was having second thoughts.

I kind of was, but for the time being I brushed them aside.

"Nope, not at all," I lied.

CHAPTER
Three

"**A**re you aware of just how haunted Pennyland is?" Jason asked with grave earnestness. He was the last kid we had to interview, and as tired as I was after a long day, this question made me sit up a little.

"Yes, of course we are," Clarice said. "That's part of the reason I wrote an entire episode set there."

Um, I hadn't been aware of just how haunted Pennyland was, but I couldn't say that. I didn't want to appear like I wasn't in the know. I'd read the script for "The Scream Queen," but it didn't give any background on the location. In the script, Pennyland was an old, abandoned amusement park on the outskirts of Winnipeg. It was haunted by an evil clown, Beauregard, and a dozen or so innocent people he had murdered. I knew the *Screamers* playbook — set the action in a real-life creepy location and weave the story around some actual legend or lore. But that's all the "true stories" were: legend and lore. Ghosts didn't exist and there was no such thing as haunted locations.

But the way Jason had spoken with such conviction made me question my beliefs, if only a little.

"I'm not talking about a couple of people who say they've heard footsteps when they were alone," Jason said with a smile that made me wonder if he was more excited about visiting Pennyland than he was about the show. "Or felt a cold draft on a hot summer day, or had the feeling they were being watched by unseen eyes. I'm talking about multiple accounts of an incredibly sinister nature from reliable eyewitnesses."

Clarice smiled but it didn't look genuine to me. "Which is why we feel this episode will be perfect for the season three premiere."

"And I couldn't agree more!" Jason practically leapt out of his chair as he said this. Now I was sure about it — he *was* more excited about ghost hunting than acting. "Many people think the most-haunted spots in the country are the Banff Springs Hotel, or the Hockey Hall of Fame, or any one of the lighthouses along the east coast. But none of those places even comes close to Pennyland. It's going to make for an epic episode. You guys are brilliant!"

Clarice's expression warmed, and even Anthony's lips upturned at the corners slightly, which was the closest I'd ever seen him come to smiling.

Jason told us it would be a dream come true for him to

act in this episode, Clarice asked a few more questions, and he and I performed the same scene I'd done with each of the other contestants. Although I felt like he was more interested in the ghosts than anything else, he was good. Maybe not Sai good, but good.

After Jason left I couldn't stop thinking about what he'd said about Pennyland, so I excused myself and ran after him. Luckily he hadn't gotten far. He was halfway down the hall, speaking with a man who I assumed was his dad. I ran to catch up.

"Hey, Jason," I said once I'd reached them.

Jason turned around and his cheeks flushed red when he saw it was me. "Oh, hey." He reached into his pocket and pulled out one of the thin balloons I'd used to tie him to the chair. "I swear I did not take this on purpose as a souvenir or anything like that and I was definitely going to mail it back to the show as soon as I got home."

"What?" I frowned, looking at the balloon. "I don't care about that. You can keep it."

He nodded in relief and returned the balloon to his pocket.

His dad hooked a thumb at me and asked his son, "Who's this clown?"

"Dad!" Jason shouted, mortified. His cheeks flushed redder than before, so red I thought his blood vessels were popping. "This is Zoë Winter! Star of Screamers."

It was Jason's dad's turn to blush. "Oh my goodness! I'm so sorry! I didn't mean to call you a *clown* clown. It's just, you're wearing clown makeup, and I thought . . ." He looked from me to his son. Jason looked like he wanted to crawl into a hole and die. "I thought . . ." He turned and pointed down the hall. "I'm just going to walk thataway. Zoë, nice to meet you. Jason, take as much time as you'd like."

"I am so sorry about that," Jason said when we were alone. "It's not every day your dad insults a celebrity."

"Don't worry about it. He was just joking around. I was actually hoping we could talk," I said. "Do you have a minute?"

Jason looked at his dad walking quickly away and said, "I do now."

The two of us found a quiet corner with a couple of chairs and sat down.

"What's up?" Jason asked. "Did I get the part? Did my dad just lose it for me?"

"Don't worry, your dad didn't hurt your chances. They haven't had time to make their final decisions, but you did well. I wanted to ask you about Pennyland. You seem to know a lot about ghosts."

"My dad showed me his old, battered VHS copy of *Ghostbusters* when I was four and I've been obsessed ever since. I've read every book by Jeremy Sinclair, both the Screamers and Haunted Coasts series — I especially love Haunted Coasts, since they're true stories. I've spent countless hours researching haunted locations online. And I've even got a bunch of ghost-hunting gear I use to conduct my own investigations. So yeah, I know a lot about ghosts."

A shiver ran up and down my spine. "Searching haunted houses in the middle of the night doesn't sound like my idea of a good time."

"It's not so bad as long as you're not alone. I've got a small group of friends who love this stuff too, so we make a night of it. Flashlights, drinks, snacks—"

"Cheese puffs?"

"Of course! No ghost hunt is complete without cheese puffs."

As good as the snacks sounded, the most appealing aspect to me was the night out with friends. Although I was a bit of a chicken when it came to real-life scary stuff, I had to admit that sounded like a lot of fun. "I can't remember the last time I did something fun like that. The last couple of years have been all work, work, work."

"Wow," Jason said, breaking eye contact with me to stare at the floor. "That's, um, kinda sad."

"I'm kidding," I said, deciding to double down on the joke. "I attended a production party last year that was pretty awesome. And just the other day I took a five-minute break and didn't think about filming or home-schooling or anything."

"You're a wild thing, Zoë."

"Let's keep that between us, okay? I have a reputation to maintain."

"Okay," Jason said with a nod. "What do you want to know about Pennyland?"

With all the talk of cheese puffs and parties and nights out with friends, I'd forgotten all about that. "Right. What makes it more haunted than those other places you mentioned?"

He eyed me as if debating how much to reveal. "A long time ago there was an accident and, well, the ghosts of Pennyland are . . . they're evil. Pure evil."

"Pure evil?" I said, feeling a small lump form in the back of my throat.

"Yeah, pure evil. Like, think of the scariest ghosts and poltergeists you've seen in horror movies — or any episode of *Screamers*, for that matter — and times that by ten."

"But ghosts can't hurt living people," I said. I laughed nervously. "What am I saying? Ghosts aren't even real."

Jason looked like he'd been slapped. "And to think I was about to invite you to tag along on one of my ghost-hunting nights."

I instantly regretted my words. "You were going to invite me out?"

His offended expression broke into a wide, mischievous smile. "I'm joking!" He smiled wider still and added, "I was never going to invite you."

He really was a pretty good actor. I'd bought his act hook, line and sinker.

Jason's phone dinged. He checked it and said, "It's my dad. He's pretty embarrassed and wants to go. Nice meeting you, Zoë."

"You too, Jason."

He turned and left. I returned to the office and rejoined Clarice and Anthony. They were studying three headshots on the table.

"Ah, there you are, Zoë," Clarice said.

"We think we've picked the winners of the contest," Anthony said.

"What do you think?" Clarice asked.

I approached the table and looked at the faces staring up at me: Sai Devan, Aaliyah Hill and Jason Lam.

"I think we've found our cast," I said.

CHAPTER
Four

The announcement of the winners made headlines across the country. The four of us were interviewed by a dozen television stations and websites. The studio booked an afternoon photo shoot so they'd have plenty of pictures they could slowly release throughout production of "The Scream Queen." I looked forward to every meeting with Sai, Aaliyah and Jason, but they were too brief. Between makeup and hair, and interviews and pictures, we hardly had any time to talk about anything other than the show. But we got along well and I was content knowing we'd soon have plenty of time to just hang out and talk and do whatever normal kids my age do. There's a famous expression people say about film and television production: Hurry up and wait.

I could wait.

And time passed. Slowly, but I was patient. My mom kept to our home-schooling schedule so that I wouldn't fall behind in my studies. I had some post-production work to do on the season two finale — just a little audio dubbing for dialogue that wasn't quite clear enough — before it aired. I had a pile of scripts to read, the first few episodes to be filmed after "The Scream Queen." My agent went into overdrive to capitalize on the buzz around the contest and lined up meetings with countless feature-film production studios. There was even interest from a music studio in having me record a solo album of dark, gothic pop songs. The only problem with that idea was I couldn't sing well enough to be the next Billie Eilish . . . or even the next Baby Shark.

That wasn't the whole truth. There was another problem. A problem with all the extra attention. It was putting any chance at having a normal life farther behind me. If the journalists could crack open my skull, peel apart the spongy wrinkles of my brain, and see the thoughts that were hidden within, they'd have a field day. I could see the headline now:

ZOË WINTER, *SCREAMERS* STAR, READY TO THROW EVERYTHING AWAY

As tempting as I had to admit that thought was, I was committed to filming a third season of *Screamers*. But I could say no to any other offers that came my way. And the more time I spent with Sai, Aaliyah and Jason, the more I was excited to get to spend a whole week on set with them at the end of August.

And then one day, a few months after I'd first met my three new co-stars, I woke up and it was finally time to fly to Winnipeg.

I picked up my phone and smiled at the photo I'd chosen for my wallpaper: a picture of the four of us from our photo shoot. I opened a group text.

Pennyland here we come! Cotton candy and carnies and clowns, oh my!

I hit send and instantly felt a little embarrassed. A new headline came to me:

CELEBRITY ZOË WINTER REVEALED TO BE HUGE DORK

The bus we were on exited the highway and headed north on a country road. The producers had offered to hire me a limousine, but I had politely turned that down and insisted on travelling from Winnipeg Richardson International Airport with the rest of the kids and the parent that had accompanied each. Aaliyah and her dad were seated across the aisle from me and my mom, Sai and his dad were behind Aaliyah, and Jason and his mom were behind me.

"So, um, how were your flights?" Glenda, the show's

production assistant, asked us all from the seat directly in front of me. Making small talk wasn't one of her fortes, but she was really good at keeping people on schedule, booking travel and hotel accommodations and making sure the entire production didn't go off the rails, which was somewhat more important than chit-chat.

Mrs. Lam, Jason's mother, swatted his arm and said, "Take off your headphones."

Jason did as he was told. "Uh, hello? I was listening to a paranormal podcast."

Mrs. Lam continued, "If someone asks you a question, it's rude not to answer. This nice young lady asked how your flight was."

After shooting his mother a slightly annoyed look, Jason said, "Fine, I guess. It's only about two hours from Edmonton to Winnipeg so I watched *The Great Fright North* on my laptop, ate some questionable airplane pizza, and here we are."

"I swear, it's like he's not even excited," Mrs. Lam said to Mr. Devan, Sai's father. "Jason, you won a free trip and a part on *Screamers*. Most kids your age would die for this opportunity!"

"I'm excited!" Jason said defensively. "I just don't like flying, okay?"

"My flight from Vancouver was only a little longer than yours," Sai said quickly, trying to breeze past the uncomfortable exchange between Jason and his mother. "It was my first flight and I really enjoyed it. I mean, it was a little difficult to focus on learning my lines since I was trapped between a loud snorer and a loud chewer. And the flight attendant skipped my row so I didn't get my free drink, but other than that, yeah . . . it was great."

Mr. Devan frowned. "Hey, wait a minute. I sat beside you . . . and I didn't eat anything . . . Do I snore?"

Sai shrugged.

"I snore," Mr. Devan said quietly to himself.

Glenda looked at Aaliyah. "How about you?"

Aaliyah had been on her phone since we first boarded the bus. "My flights were perfect," she said without taking her eyes off her screen. "You can see all the highlights on my Instagram."

"Are you posting to Instagram right now?" Glenda asked.

"Not exclusively," Aaliyah said. "I've also posted on TikTok."

"My daughter is very good on the internet," Mr. Hill said. "She's going to be a famous social media influence one day."

"Influencer, Dad," Aaliyah said, her tone patient and kind.

"Wait," Jason said. "Did you say *flights*?"

Aaliyah nodded. "St. John's to Montreal to Toronto to here. Took about twelve hours."

Jason looked appalled. "And spending half a day trapped

on planes and in airports is your idea of *perfect*?"

"I'm never alone when I've got this," Aaliyah said, giving her phone a little shake in the air.

"I was there too," Mr. Hill said, with a slightly sad shrug.

"All right, well, I'm glad to hear your flights were . . . flights." Glenda frowned as if realizing how awkward she sounded, and then, without saying anything else, she turned to face forward and sat back down. I heard her sigh loudly.

As I watched Aaliyah continue to tap away on her phone, I felt a hint of dread. *I hope she didn't post any pictures of me. What if she has thousands, or tens of thousands, of followers?*

"This is exciting, isn't it?" Mom said. "Filming an episode with three new kids?"

I nodded. It was, but I also had a sudden bad feeling in the pit of my stomach. Something I couldn't fully explain. Was the quinoa I'd eaten on the plane upsetting my digestion? Yes, that must have been it. Bad quinoa.

"What is it, sweetheart?" Mom asked. She could always read my expression and tell when I was hiding something.

"I don't know," I said truthfully. "Have you ever had a feeling you couldn't quite explain? A hunch, or a . . ."

"A sixth sense?" Mom said, finishing my sentence. She had a habit of doing that.

"Exactly. An intuition that says something's not right. That's what I just felt. Have you ever had that?"

She laughed gently. "No. I haven't. Sounds like something out of a *Screamers* episode, not real life. It was probably just that quinoa you ate. It smelled a little off."

"Why didn't you say so *before* I ate it?" I smiled to show her I was kidding, but the smile masked my emotions. The bad feeling — the sixth sense — hadn't gone away, and I didn't actually believe it was the quinoa.

We drove for twenty-five minutes through the country, leaving civilization farther behind with every kilometre. We hadn't passed a single building — or even another vehicle — for five minutes when our driver turned onto a dirt road so overgrown with low-hanging trees and thick bushes that it was nearly invisible, unless you knew where to look for it.

"Wait a minute," I said, tapping Glenda on the shoulder. "We're not going to the hotel?"

Glenda stood up and turned to face us with a smile. "Took you long enough."

"Long enough to *what*?" Aaliyah said, finally taking her eyes off her phone.

"To figure out something's up," Glenda said.

"Glenda!" I exclaimed. "Just tell us!"

"You four and your parents won't be staying at any run-of-the-mill hotel," Glenda said. "We have a private luxury trailer for each of you right here on set! Surprise!"

We bounced up and down as the bus drove through a

giant pothole and Glenda half sat, half fell back into her seat. I shouted excitedly, feeling a little like I was on a ride and pumped by Glenda's news, and the other kids joined me. But we all fell silent as the bus approached a faded rotting, wooden sign.

"Look at that," I told the others.

WELCOME TO PENNYLAND
HOME OF THE BIG THRILL!

Someone had spray-painted a line through THE BIG THRILL and written BEAUREGARD beneath it.

The bad feeling I'd had before came rushing back, and this time it was accompanied by a premonition: something bad was going to happen here.

CHAPTER
Five

"**I** can't believe it," Jason said quietly. He looked like he was on the verge of tears. He pulled out a camera — not a phone, but an actual camera, with buttons and knobs and a big lens and everything — and snapped a bunch of pictures of the sign through his window. It made that old-fashioned camera sound every time he pressed the button. *Ka-CHICK! Ka-CHICK! Ka-CHICK!*

"Creepy," I said, keeping my eyes glued to the sign until we had passed it.

"Vandalism is so disrespectful," Jason said. "Some people just don't respect abandoned places."

"Not abandoned," Glenda interjected.

"What's that?" Jason asked.

"Pennyland isn't abandoned. At least not anymore. It used to be, but now the rides are being restored and it's opening up again."

The bus turned a corner and entered a wide clearing into

what appeared to be a parking lot. Knee-high weeds grew through cracks in the pavement and I saw a few painted lines that were nearly completely faded away by a mixture of sun, snow and time. There were cars, trucks, film trailers and a large white tent. We pulled up in front of a row of red-and-white ticket booths. A large sign above the booths read PENNYLAN, the D missing.

"Pennyland? More like *Half*pennyland," the driver said with a chuckle.

No one laughed.

"Tough crowd," he said. He opened the door and got out of the bus, then opened the baggage-compartment doors and dumped our luggage in the dirt unceremoniously.

"I can't believe we get to sleep in an amusement park," Mom said. "Seriously, who gets to do that? It's every kid's dream, right?"

I nodded and smiled but something was preventing me from being as excited as everyone else.

We got off the bus and milled around our luggage. The driver got back on the bus without a word, closed the door, and drove off.

Zoë . . .

It sounded like someone had called my name from within Pennyland. Just a trick of the wind, but I felt something pulling me, like a magnet, toward the front gate. The bad feeling had been replaced by the desire to run past the ticket booths and into the park. I wanted to eat junk food. I wanted to go on the rides. I wanted to watch the shows. I wanted to laugh until it hurt.

"Don't worry about your bags," Glenda said, jostling me out of my thoughts. "I'll have someone take them to your trailers." She pointed at the vehicles in the parking lot. "Dinner is at eighteen hundred in that large tent." She pointed to one of the white tents in the parking lot. "And there's a welcome meeting at nineteen hundred, but other than that your afternoon is free."

"Eighteen hundred?" Sai whispered beside me.

"Military time," I whispered back. "She always does that. I'll teach you later."

"So we can check out the park?" Jason asked.

Glenda nodded. "Sure. Just don't touch anything. The crew has been here for days setting up equipment and lights and preparing the shooting locations."

Jason laughed, a sound full of mischief. He unzipped his suitcase and hastily filled his backpack with a bunch of tech gear.

"I'm going to get so many great selfies here," Aaliyah said. "Zoë, we should totally take a picture together under that Pennyland sign. We could both share it and see who gets more likes!"

I tried to smile but could only manage a smirk.

"Kidding!" Aaliyah said. "Obviously you'd get more likes."

"Thanks," I said. "But I'm okay."

Aaliyah shrugged as Sai looked hesitantly at Pennyland, then his suitcase, then the trailers, shifting his weight from foot to foot like a kid who can't decide what he wants to do.

Mr. Devan held up a finger and shook it side to side. "No, no, no. You're going with them. You spend enough time alone indoors as it is. A little fresh air and time with kids your own age will be good for you."

"But," Sai said, trying to keep his voice low enough that we wouldn't hear, "I could use the time to go over my lines."

"You've been going over your lines all day every day for a week!" Mr. Devan said. "If you haven't memorized them by now, then all those acting lessons I've paid for over the years have been a waste of money. Go! Have fun! Do normal kid stuff!"

Do normal kid stuff. Was Sai more like me than I had realized?

"Well, what are we waiting for?" I said to the other kids. "Let's go!"

I didn't have to ask Jason or Aaliyah twice. They were immediately by my side, one armed with what appeared to be a bunch of amateur ghost-hunting gear, the other armed with her phone.

Sai took one last longing look at the trailers, then joined us.

"Be safe," Mom said.

"We will be," I assured her. "How much trouble could we get into in a place like this?"

Mom opened her mouth to answer but I cut her off. "Don't answer that. Bye!"

"Remember," Glenda said, "dinner, eighteen hundred, white tent."

I turned and walked away. The other three kids followed close behind, hustling a little to keep up with my pace. "Sorry, Glenda," I called over my shoulder in a joking tone. "I didn't quite catch that."

She took the bait, sounding less composed than normal and slightly flustered. "Dinner! Eighteen hundred! White tent!"

The four of us exchanged looks and laughed. A warm and happy feeling spread through my limbs.

"I still don't know what time dinner is," Sai said. We laughed at that too.

We passed an old-fashioned ticket booth filled with dirt and debris and cobwebs, walked beneath the PENNYLAND sign that was in need of some TLC, and the park in all its glory revealed itself to us.

"Whoa," I said.

Sai whistled in awe.

Jason said, "I didn't expect it to look anything like this."

Aaliyah switched from taking photos to recording video. "I'm finally here in Pennyland and, well, check it out." She panned her phone from left to right, taking in all the sights.

The abandoned amusement park was in remarkably good shape. There was a main path that appeared to encircle Pennyland, giving guests the option of turning left or right from the entrance, walking in a big loop, and seeing everything there was to see. There were several small rides and show buildings scattered throughout the property, as well as restaurants and gift shops. To our left an impressively large but rickety-looking wooden roller coaster track stood out from the other attractions, with a tall sign identifying it as DEATH DEFLYER. To our right was a large Ferris wheel with letters affixed to its centre that read THE BIG THRILL. And straight ahead in the dead centre of the park was a circus tent that resembled a giant peppermint candy with red-and-white stripes. Members of the film crew were hard at work carting equipment around and setting things up for the following day.

Other than the people, it was like time had been frozen in Pennyland. I felt like I was looking at a picture of the park, an old postcard, not the real thing.

"It looks like it closed weeks ago, not years," I said. "How long, exactly, has this place been abandoned?"

"More than seventy years," Jason said. "I've seen pictures online that were posted a few years ago and it looked *rough*."

"Seventy years?" Aaliyah said. "How is that possible? It

should look like, well, what Jason said. Rough."

"Glenda said the park is getting restored to reopen, remember?" Sai said. "Obviously someone's been busy."

"That roller coaster looks like it might still work," Jason said.

"The Ferris wheel too," Aaliyah said. "But looks can be deceiving."

When no one responded, Aaliyah added, "I wouldn't recommend looking for the power switch and going for an unsanctioned ride, is what I'm saying."

I couldn't argue with her logic.

But Jason could. "Aaliyah, you're a genius." He ran to the circus tent and we followed. "This looks like a power switch," he said, pointing at a large metal box that was surrounded by bushes. "Who wants to go for a ride?" He placed his backpack down and grabbed the side of the box as if he was about to pull a lever.

"I said *not* to do that!" Aaliyah yelled.

"And Glenda said not to touch anything!" Sai added.

Jason started laughing and I quickly realized he was joking. "Oh man, you should've seen the looks on your faces. This isn't the main power switch. There's no way they'd have that out in the open for anyone to mess around with."

"I knew that," Sai said, still looking a little shaken.

At the same time Aaliyah said, "Ha, ha, very funny. Can we carry on now?"

"Sure thing," Jason said, bending down to pick up his backpack. He paused, then crouched low, staring through the bushes. "Hey, guys. There's something hidden in here."

"If you think you're going to make me fall for another joke so soon . . ." Aaliyah said.

"I'm not joking," Jason said. He crept forward on his hands and knees. "There's definitely something in these bushes. Or is it . . . some*one*?"

I approached slowly and peered over Jason's shoulder, my heartbeat picking up speed. What was I afraid of? It was probably nothing. Or another joke, despite what Jason said. Or his imagination.

He bent a few branches and I finally saw what he saw.

Someone screamed, a piercing sound that pained my eardrums. It took me a moment to realize that the scream-er was me.

CHAPTER
Six

I stopped screaming and instantly felt incredibly silly and embarrassed.

There was a clown staring out at us from the bushes, but not a real one. It was a full-size wooden cut-out of a clown, and a pretty realistic-looking one. But the paint was faded and the wood was covered in small patches of moss, which made the clown look even creepier.

Jason reached through the branches and pulled the clown out.

"What are you doing, man?" Sai said. "Glenda said—"

"Not to touch anything," Jason said. "Yeah, I know, but this doesn't count. Before I spotted it no one even knew it was hidden here."

"What if it's a prop for the show?" Sai said.

"Hidden in the bushes?" Jason asked. "I don't think so. Plus, you can tell it's really old, and not just made to look old. That's authentic damage from the elements," he said, pointing at various parts of the cut-out. "The *Screamers* props and sets are good, but they're not that good. No offence," he added, looking at me.

"None taken," I said distractedly. I was only half listening. I couldn't look away from the clown. It was like our eyes were locked, and then his eyes suddenly flickered. No, they couldn't have. They were nothing but two small circles of red paint.

The clown wore a billowing black gown with three large white buttons on the chest and a wide collar that looked like a giant honey-crueller doughnut around his neck. His face was coated in white paint, his mouth was excessively large and red, and he had a thin, vertical black line painted over each eye. He was bald other than three tufts of red hair.

And he held a banner at his side with words painted in large, red circus letters.

DON'T MISS
THE ONE AND ONLY
BEAUREGARD
HE LAUGHS!
HE CRIES!
HE'S A RIOT!
LIVE PERFORMANCES EVERY NIGHT AT SUNDOWN

So this was Beauregard, the clown I'd played during our screen tests and the villain of this episode. The clown that was believed to haunt the park.

"I don't know about you guys," Aaliyah said, "but I'm starting to wish I could still catch one of Beauregard's shows."

"Why?" Sai asked.

"He's a riot!" Aaliyah said excitedly.

"And that's a good thing?" Sai said.

Aaliyah shrugged. "I don't know. I think so. Maybe. If anything it means his shows weren't boring, right?"

"One thing's for sure," Jason said. "Beauregard's death has made his shows a lot more exciting." He chuckled.

Sai and Aaliyah stared at Jason, utterly confused.

"Oh, right! I only told her," Jason said, pointing at me. "Um, 'The Scream Queen' is based on the true legend of Beauregard. Some believe he killed people before he died, and others believe he's still capable of killing people."

Neither Sai nor Aaliyah said anything. Instead, they stared at each other, then at me, then back at Jason.

"Allegedly. You know, if you believe in that sort of thing," Jason said with a wave of his hand meant to brush off the seriousness of his words. "I'm sure the rumours aren't true." He raised his hand to block his face from the others' view and mouthed, "The rumours are totally true," to me.

"So, wait," Aaliyah said, pointing at the cut-out. "You're

telling me a clown — this clown, the clown in our episode — haunts Pennyland?"

Jason nodded. "That's what I'm telling you."

Just when I thought Aaliyah might freak out, she said, "That's so sick! If I could get a picture of a real-life ghost — or better yet, *with* a real-life ghost — it would go viral!"

"I want to get a picture of Beauregard or one of the other ghosts too," Jason said, slinging his backpack over his shoulder. "I brought a bunch of my gear. I'm kind of an amateur ghost hunter."

"Hold on a minute," Sai said, putting a hand to his forehead as if he felt a headache coming on. "Did you say *other* ghosts? As in, there's more than one?"

"I did," Jason said with a nod. "There's Beauregard. They say he snapped and killed a bunch of people. And there was also an accident involving The Big Thrill — the Ferris wheel — sometime in the 1920s or 30s. The people who died haven't been able to move on. Again, allegedly, but I want to find out for sure."

"Am I the only one of who wants nothing to do with these *alleged* ghosts?" Sai asked in disbelief. "What about you, Zoë?"

Being scared on set by fake ghosts hadn't made me any braver, and the thought of coming face to face with a real ghost still terrified me. But then I recalled what Jason had said back in Toronto about his friends, their ghost hunts and the cheese puffs . . . "I don't know, searching for real ghosts does sound like it could be fun."

Sai raised his hands in defeat. "I'm the only person here who has any sense. I wasn't even afraid of clowns before today, but I feel like this is a good time and place to start."

"I won't disagree with that, Sai," I said, taking the cut-out from Jason. The temperature seemed to drop a few degrees and a thin trail of mist snaked around my feet.

"What are you doing?" Jason asked.

"I'm putting Beauregard back where he belongs," I said. "Hidden in the bushes. Out of sight, out of mind." The clown's red eyes seemed to flicker again, sending a shiver up my spine.

"Don't touch that!" someone commanded behind us.

Oh no, I thought. Maybe the cut-out was a prop after all.

But when we turned around, we found the person who had spoken wasn't part of the crew. It was a boy. He was with a girl. Both of them were a few years older than us and dressed in old-fashioned clothing. They stood ankle-deep in a pool of mist.

They're extras, I thought. People hired to appear in the background of crowd scenes.

But why were they in costume a day early? And why were they in old-fashioned costumes?

"I'm . . ." I was momentarily lost for words. My mind was screaming that everything about this was off, that something about this was bad, that there was no reason for them to care what we were doing. But I was too polite, I guess, to dodge the question, and answered truthfully. It's not like I had anything to hide and we hadn't done anything wrong. "I'm putting this sign back where we found it."

"You shouldn't have touched that," the girl hissed.

"Okay, let's not overreact," I said, trying to remain calm but feeling my heart beat a little harder. "It's just an old sign."

Beside me, Jason slowly reached into his backpack and pulled out a gadget that looked like a remote control. It was black with orange buttons and had a digital screen.

Something about him doing that freaked me out, big time. Alarm bells went off in my head as goosebumps coated the skin of my arms. I shared a look with Sai and Aaliyah, and both looked as concerned as I was beginning to feel.

"It's not just an old sign," the boy said.

"Not to him," the girl added as she pointed at Beauregard's cut-out.

The mist swirled around their feet and wound around their knees, then their waists, then their chests.

They weren't extras . . .

They were ghosts.

Jason's eyes widened as he stared at his gadget.

"Unbelievable," he said with a smile.

"He is not going to be happy," Ghost Boy said.

"He is going to be angry with you," Ghost Girl said, pointing at us.

Ghost Girl's words struck me in the middle of the chest and spread an icy cold blast through my entire body. My knees felt weak and I was afraid I might fall over.

"And when he's angry with you—" Ghost Boy said.

"You're as good as dead," Ghost Girl finished.

My breath caught in my throat and I had to struggle for air.

Jason quickly reached into his backpack and grabbed a video camera, but he was too late to record any footage.

The mist wrapped around the couple's faces, seeping into their mouths and noses and eyes and completely obscuring them from view. Half a heartbeat later the mist dissipated. The ghosts were gone.

CHAPTER
Seven

"**W**hat was that?" Sai yelled. "What just happened?"

I shushed him. "Keep your voice down." Three crew members wheeling a cart of boxes were approaching us.

"Is this really the time to shush me?" Sai asked. "We just saw two ghosts. And they warned us about another ghost. And then the mist *ate them!*"

"I get that you're freaking out," I said, placing my hands on his shoulders to calm him down. "Trust me, I'm freaking out too. But let me tell you something I've learned from experience. Television producers are nervous people. Like, all the time. They don't *breathe* until they're sure it's their best course of action. So if they hear about what just happened, and if they think that Pennyland is actually haunted, they might move the production, or delay it, or worst of all, cancel it. And I know you wouldn't want that."

Sai stopped shaking and took a deep breath, then nodded. "You're right. I wouldn't want that. I'm sorry for panicking, but it's not every day you see a couple of dead people disappear before your eyes."

Aaliyah sighed and said, "I can't believe I didn't get a picture of them. Or *with* them."

Jason shoved his camera back into his bag. "I didn't get any pictures of them either!"

"*Ixnay* on the *ostsghay*," I whispered harshly. The three crew members were close.

"Icky on the what-now?" Aaliyah said, her face scrunched up.

"It's pig Latin. No ghost talk!" I turned around and waved at the crew members with a nice big smile as they passed. "Hey, guys! Setting up for the big day tomorrow, eh?"

The first two men nodded politely and carried on, but the third hung back and approached me hesitantly.

"I'm sorry to bother you, uh, Ms. Winter, but I heard—"

Oh no, I thought, feeling my stomach dip and dive. *He heard us! He knows!*

"—that you don't mind signing autographs?"

"Oh," I said, feeling a great deal of relief and a small dash of embarrassment overtake the turmoil in my gut. "Sure. Of course."

The man smiled, reached into his pocket, and handed me a small notebook and pencil.

I pressed the pencil tip to the paper and paused. "Should I make it out to you?"

"What?" the man said, taking off his baseball cap and running his grimy fingers through his balding hair. "No, it's not for me. It's for my daughter, Julie. She's twelve."

"Right," I said, feeling a little embarrassed. "To Julie, then." Under her name I wrote my catchphrase:

Try not to SCREAM!

xo Zoë Winter

The man thanked me and hurried to catch up with the other crew members.

"Good job, Zoë," Aaliyah said.

"Thanks, I guess," I said. At first I thought she was teasing me, but on second thought I didn't believe she was. "But the next crew member or extra who walks past might not have a twelve-year-old daughter who wants an autograph, and they might overhear what we're saying. We have to be more careful."

The others exchanged looks and nodded. It was obvious to me why they were willing to play along. Sai didn't want to miss his big acting break, Aaliyah didn't want to see her door to fame slam shut and Jason wanted to play *Ghostbusters*.

And me? I didn't want to lose my new friends as soon as I'd made them. As creepy as the kids in the mist had been, it's not like they had attacked us. And although they said

Beauregard would be angry, it's not like ghosts could actually hurt the living.

Could they?

I was pretty sure they couldn't.

I'd have to ask Jason.

Or not. Maybe it was better not to know.

"Cool," I said, wanting to change the subject . . . and the direction my thoughts were headed. "This is a big amusement park and so far we've seen very little of it. Why don't we go explore some more before dinner?"

"I like that idea," Sai said with a nod so vigorous I was afraid he'd give himself whiplash. "I like that idea *a lot*. Let's put the ghosts in the past and move on."

We started walking — Death Deflyer's highest peak looming ahead of us.

"Technically speaking," Jason said, "all ghosts are in the past — or at least *from* the past — because they can't move on. But I get your point, and don't worry — I'll be prepared next time and give everyone as much warning as possible if I pick up on anything unusual." He pulled his remote thingy back out of his backpack and turned it on.

"Good," Aaliyah said. "I'm not leaving this park at the end of the week without a picture of a real-life Casper."

"Except Casper's friendly," Jason said. "The ghosts here are . . ." He trailed off upon noticing the concerned look on Sai's face. ". . . perfectly lovely, I'm sure."

Sai swallowed and shook his head. It didn't look like he was buying what Jason was selling.

"Don't worry. With any luck, the ghosts here will find their way to the Netherrealm," Jason reassured Sai.

"What's the Netherrealm? And how do you get ghosts to go there?" I asked.

"You don't," Jason said. "It would be nearly impossible to force a ghost with unfinished business to leave this plane."

"There must be something that holds power over ghosts," Aaliyah said.

Jason nodded. "There is. Iron, certain rocks, salt, totems like horseshoes. Some people also believe ghosts' names hold a little power over them. But if a spirit truly wants to stay here, chances are it's staying as long as it wants."

We passed a bunch of kiddie rides and small attractions with names like Shimmy and Caterpillar and Flying Saucer, as well as a carousel with circus animals for riders to sit on. Everything was lit up and some of the rides were being tested. What drew us forward was Death Deflyer.

"Think it still works?" Aaliyah asked.

"I hope so," Jason said. "I love coasters."

"Glenda said they're fixing up all the rides," I said. There was no one working on the coaster but maybe it was already complete. There was a climactic scene in "The Scream Queen" in which Aaliyah and I rode The Big Thrill while the boys rode Death Deflyer, and we watched helplessly as Beauregard's ghost appeared in the seat behind them — but that was going to be filmed in front of a green screen, not on the actual rides.

"I wouldn't ride it for a million bucks," Sai said.

"Chicken," Jason teased.

"That's one word," Sai said. "Another is intelligent. And I'm smart enough to have a healthy respect for heights."

"Do you mean a *fear* of heights?" Jason asked.

"Same thing," Sai said.

The roller coaster track towered over everything else on this side of the park. It ran east — past the back of the circus tent, near the Ferris wheel, and back again. It was ancient looking — constructed of wooden beams with a steel track. The passenger cars in the loading station were painted bright red, green, yellow and blue, and their seats had safety bars that would be lowered over riders' laps. The track climbed to a dizzying height that must have been nearly thirty metres tall, then plunged down before reaching the second hill. It wasn't the tallest roller coaster I'd ever seen, and it didn't have any loops or corkscrews, but it scared me far more than any coaster I'd ridden. The new ones were constructed of steel beams and supports, held you securely in place with over-the-shoulder restraints and were as smooth as butter. But Death Deflyer? The wood might be rotting, the whole track might come crashing down with the gentlest of breezes, and all that separated you from certain death was a small metal bar on your lap.

"You're wondering who you have to bribe to get a ride, aren't you?" someone asked from behind us.

We turned around and saw a middle-aged woman watching us with a wide smile. She wore a grey jumpsuit that was covered in dirt and grease. Below the words "Active Attractions" was a sewn-on name tag that said BETH.

"My name's Harriett," she said.

"But . . . that says Beth," I said, pointing at her name tag.

"Right!" Harriett said. "I keep forgetting that. This isn't my uniform. Well, it is now, but it wasn't always. I'm the head ride technician. I took over from Beth not too long ago. And she took over from some guy who took over from a few other guys. No one's stayed in this position for long . . ." She frowned, then brightened and added with a laugh, "Maybe the job is cursed!"

Maybe this whole amusement park is cursed, I thought. "Did you ask us if we want to ride . . ." I pointed at Death Deflyer as a gentle breeze made it sway and groan. ". . . that death trap? You don't even know who we are!"

Harriett nodded, her smile no less warm and sincere. "You're here with that show, *Shivers*. I met a woman yesterday — I think she said she was a director. Clarette? And she told me four kids your age would be coming by today. I don't see any other kids around here."

I opened my mouth to correct Harriett on the name of the show and the director, but then thought, *What's the point?* Her name tag had a different woman's name on it, so she obviously didn't care too much about details . . . a concerning thought, given her job.

Harriett continued. "I can tell you all want to hop on Death Deflyer right now, but you're going to have to hold your horses — she's not running."

"Ah, well, that's a—" Sai started to say before Harriett bulldozed on.

"Yet. She's not running yet."

"Relief," Sai said, finishing his sentence. "I was going to say that's a relief, but never mind."

If Harriett had heard Sai, she paid him no attention. "But she will be running tomorrow come H-E double hockey sticks or high water, or my name ain't Harriett. Or even Beth." She laughed like she'd just told the funniest joke in the world. "We've been testing it with barrels of water and crash-test dummies, and early tomorrow morning we're going to test it with some junior Pennyland employees, and then — assuming there aren't any, uh, accidents — then . . ." Harriett pointed at us in a way that looked like she was trying to be coy, but to me it came off as threatening. "Then you four are in for the ride of your life."

CHAPTER
Eight

Harriett waved good-naturedly as we walked away. I looked back at her a few times, half expecting her to disappear in a cloud of mist.

"Hey, Jason," I said. "Any chance she was, you know . . . ?"

"A ghost?" he asked. "No, she was an odd duck but definitely not dead."

"How can you be sure?" I asked.

He held up his black-and-orange gadget. "Because of this."

"What is that, anyway?" Aaliyah asked. "Some sort of ancient cellphone from prehistoric times or something?"

"No, it's an EMF sensor. It registers excess electromagnetic radiation in the atmosphere, which could be a sign that a ghost is nearby. And the reading was normal the whole time we talked with Beth."

"Harriett," Sai corrected.

"Right," Jason said.

"Do you really think her job could be cursed? Is that even a thing?" Aaliyah asked.

"I thought the same thing!" I said. "Like, maybe the job isn't cursed, but this whole place is."

"Or maybe people who work here get too scared and quit," Jason said. "All the way back to the guy who took over for a bunch of other guys, and then Harriett."

"Beth," Sai corrected.

"Right," Jason said.

"Either way," Sai said, "there's no way we're going to take Harriett up on her offer to ride Death Deflyer, right?"

No one answered.

"Seriously?" Sai said, incredulous.

"I love roller coasters!" Jason said.

"What would my followers think if I *didn't* ride it?" Aaliyah said.

I hadn't ridden a roller coaster in years. The simple act of going to an amusement park hadn't been possible since *Screamers* became a smash hit. I was recognized every time I took five steps and then asked for autographs and pictures, making it nearly impossible to do anything in public.

But here, in Pennyland . . . there were no lineups, no crowds, no one asking me for an autograph other than the occasional crew member and no one wanting to take my picture, other than Aaliyah. It was paradise. With ghosts. But paradise nonetheless.

Sai was still looking at me expectantly.

I shrugged in response.

"Once again I'm reminded that I'm the only one with any sense among us," Sai said. "You can all die on the coaster if you like but I'll just watch from the ground, thank you."

"Sounds like a plan, Dad," Jason said.

Sai sighed but dropped the subject, and we carried on. We passed a few more small rides, a couple of midway games and a restaurant called Excitement Eats before nearing the back of the circus tent in the middle of the park. At first I'd thought it was made of canvas, but upon closer inspection I realized it was constructed of some sort of solid material, like concrete or metal, and painted to look like a classic circus tent.

"Check that out!" Aaliyah said.

She pointed at a building attached to the back of the tent. It appeared to be a funhouse. It was two storeys high and painted in red-and-white stripes too. But the feature that commanded my attention was the entrance. It was a giant clown face, and the door was inside the clown's wide-open mouth. Above the clown's curly orange hair was a sign that read THE LAFFIN' PLACE.

"Awesome!" Jason said. He looked pleadingly at Sai and cupped his hands together as if begging. "Can we go inside, Dad? Pretty please with sugar on top?"

"I might be ten times more mature than you but that

doesn't make me your dad," Sai said. He looked at his watch. "But it's getting late. I think we should hurry to get back in time for dinner." He looked at me to back him up.

"Sai's right," I said. "It's almost eighteen hundred and we can't be late for our first meal and production meeting."

"I am hungry," Jason said, patting his belly while looking longingly at The Laffin' Place. "I'll come back to you later," he promised the clown.

We were drawn toward the park's other focal point, The Big Thrill. The Ferris wheel was impressively large and had twenty-four cabins to ride in.

"Hmm," Jason said as we approached the ride.

"What is it?" I asked.

"Probably nothing," he said without taking his eyes off his EMF sensor, "but I'm getting a higher reading than usual."

"Is it a ghost?" Sai asked, looking around frantically.

"Yeah, it's a ghost — that's why I said it's probably nothing," Jason said dryly. "But this is where I assume the ghosts we saw earlier spend most of their time."

"Why?" I asked.

"The rumoured accident happened here, on The Big Thrill."

"The Ferris wheel killed a bunch of people?" Aaliyah asked in surprise.

Jason nodded. "Allegedly, yeah."

"How?" Sai asked.

"There are a lot of different stories on the internet, but most say that a number of cabins came loose from their moorings and slid back and forth as the wheel revolved, then crashed to the ground from the peak of the ride."

"Do you believe that?" I asked.

"Well, it's the internet, so no, not really. But a lot of people do, and the electromagnetic reading here is still creeping up and up . . ."

"Isn't it enough that I already told you four you could ride Death Deflyer?"

I spun around. It was Harriett again, standing just a metre or two away from us. Was she following us?

"Beth!" Jason said, startled.

"Harriett," Sai corrected for a third time.

"Call me either," Harriett said with a smile so big it forced her eyes shut. "Just don't call me late for dinner."

The other kids and I looked at one another, no one sure what to say to that.

"Isn't she a beaut?" Harriett said as she admired The Big Thrill. "About a century old and still runs like a dream. We added a few enhancements to make her a little more, well, thrilling. Modern-day riders wouldn't be happy if they went on a ride with the word 'thrill' in it if it didn't have a few thrills, amirite?"

I didn't quite know what to say to that either. "I guess

not. Say, Harriett, do you know anything about an accident on The Big Thrill?"

"You betcha! There was blood and guts and body parts all over the ride!"

"Really?" Jason, Sai and Aaliyah asked together in a rousing chorus of shock. I'd lost the ability to talk.

"No!" Harriett barked a laugh and pointed at us. "But you should have seen the looks on your faces. Classic."

"You see, Jason?" Sai said. "No accident."

"Oh, there was an accident," Harriett said.

"Huh?" I asked. "But you said—"

"I said no, there wasn't any blood or guts or body parts on the ride, but that's only because the blood and guts and body parts would've been cleaned up a long, long time ago."

"So there was an accident on The Big Thrill?" Jason asked excitedly. "And people were killed?"

"That's what I've heard," Harriett said. "Some even say the place is haunted. The staff talk about stuff they've heard, felt . . . even seen. But who knows what to believe. I haven't had a single paranormal encounter the entire time I've worked here."

"How long have you worked here?" I asked her.

"Three whole days," Harriett said, then her eyes widened, her mouth gaped open, and she pointed somewhere behind us. "What's that?!"

I spun around expecting to see another ghost in

old-fashioned clothing, but all I saw was The Laffin' Place, some film-crew members and some Pennyland employees in reflective vests and hard hats.

"Made you look." Harriett had a mischievous twinkle in her eye that made her look fourteen, not forty-whatever-she-was. "Remember, there's no such thing as ghosts. Not here, not anywhere. See you all tomorrow for those rides." She tipped her hard hat and sauntered off.

"Does that woman do any actual work?" Aaliyah asked. "Or does she just walk around chatting with strangers?"

"One thing's for sure," Jason said. "She fits in well around here. Both she and Pennyland are a little weird."

"We should go," I said. "It's almost dinnertime."

"Dinner. Finally, something I understand," Sai said. "Followed by the production meeting." He looked as excited by that prospect as a kid on Christmas morning.

We began walking. A cold breeze drifted through the park and made me shiver. I stuck my hands in my armpits to keep them warm and stole a glance over my shoulder. No Harriett.

But there was someone else, someone I hadn't seen before, standing in the shadows of The Laffin' Place, watching.

A clown.

I blinked . . .

And he was gone.

CHAPTER
Nine

I'd never been so happy to be hanging out in a parking lot.

As soon as we passed through the front gate, I felt a sense of relief, and I realized a bad feeling had been lingering in my gut from the time the two ghosts had accosted us in front of the tent.

That wasn't Beauregard, I tried to assure myself. But who, or what, was it? A park employee? An actor in a clown costume? Or a figment of my imagination?

I could live with any of those explanations. The alternative — that it actually had been Beauregard — was incomprehensible and terrifying.

Or it would've been incomprehensible before that day, but now I knew ghosts were real. It was still a terrifying and dangerous possibility.

Although we were among the last members of the cast and crew to enter the parking-lot tent where dinner was being served, there was still no shortage of food. There were five rows of plastic folding tables and chairs filled with people eating and talking excitedly — there was always a buzz in the air at the first meal once the cast and crew had all arrived on set.

I spotted Mom — she was sitting at a table with the other parents — and we waved to each other. She looked happy, and that made me happy.

Jason, Sai and Aaliyah eyed the buffet like little kids in a candy shop. There was pizza, chicken, hamburgers, fish, vegan wraps and a dozen side dishes. To the left was a soup and salad bar, and to the right was a sundae bar.

"It's beautiful," Aaliyah said softly as we sat down at an available table. Their plates were piled high.

"It's like I've died and gone to heaven," Jason said.

"I'm going to eat so much that I'll never be able to eat again," Sai said.

"Pace yourselves," I cautioned. "It's like this at every meal."

The boys didn't heed my words and began shovelling food into their mouths like a couple of starved wolves. Aaliyah paused only long enough to take a few pictures of her food and post them to her social media accounts before digging in with as much gusto as Jason and Sai. I wished I could enjoy my food as much as the others.

"Aren't you hungry?" Aaliyah asked.

"Not really," I said with a smile. "It's not every day you

see your first ghost. And your second." *And your third,* I thought.

Aaliyah set her fork down. "Oh yeah. I forgot about that."

"Me too." Sai pushed his plate away. "But now I've lost my appetite."

"You going to finish those fries?" Jason asked Sai as he crammed another taco in his mouth.

"You've probably seen countless ghosts before," I said to Jason, which is how I assumed he could still eat.

He shook his head. "Nah. Believe it or not, those were my first. Most ghost hunts produce little more than some odd atmospheric readings or a hint of a whisper on an audio recording that might only be someone opening a pack of Skittles. Turns out, seeing ghosts works up quite an appetite in me. Ooh, speaking of Skittles, I think it's about time for dessert."

Twenty-five minutes later, once Jason had thrown in the towel halfway through his third ice-cream sundae, Clarice and Glenda stood up and approached a microphone that had been set up in the corner of the tent.

"Good evening, everyone," Glenda said. "I hope you all enjoyed dinner. For anyone who doesn't yet know me, my name is Glenda and I'm the production assistant for *Screamers,* so it's my job to keep the production on schedule. It's also my job tonight to introduce this episode's director, Clarice Stallard."

There was a round of applause as Clarice smiled and stepped up to the mic.

"Thank you, everyone, thank you," Clarice said. "I'll keep this brief since I don't think all of you have had the chance to visit the sundae bar yet and I'm all that's standing between it and you."

Amidst some laughs from the audience, Jason held his stomach and slumped a little in his seat. "I don't feel so hot," he said.

Clarice continued. "I've had the pleasure of working with some of you before on previous episodes, and I've enjoyed every moment on the *Screamers* set. But this episode is extra special to me. Not only is it the fiftieth episode, and next season's premiere, but it's also the script I'm most proud of."

My heart swelled with joy for Clarice. She'd been writing for the show since the beginning and had directed five episodes. And she was as kind and generous as she was talented. We'd bonded from the first time we met, and the scripts she'd written kept having bigger and better roles for me — which was great for my career, but made things awkward between me and the other actors.

In this one I played a character named Chloe Summer (she'd written this script just for me), who wins a contest to be the first kid, along with her three closest friends, to visit a new amusement park before it opens to the public.

My character is thrilled, but her excitement is short-lived as she and her friends soon discover the park is haunted by the ghost of a murderous clown and a host of people the clown had killed long ago. The script was packed with action and scares and a whole bunch of paranormal stuff I'd never heard of before — time slips and fetches — but the best part was the twist ending. At the very end, Chloe thinks she has saved her friends from the ghost clown, only to see the entire world transform before her eyes. She hasn't been in an amusement park but a psychiatric hospital all along. Her friends don't even know her — they're other patients. And the head doctor looks just like the clown, minus the face paint and silly outfit. Chloe screams, and . . . cut to black.

Thinking of the storyline as Clarice gave her speech, I suddenly felt a little sick. The script was beginning to imitate my life, or was that the other way around? I didn't want to end up like Chloe. Scared, delusional, trapped in a hospital, being treated by a doctor that looked just like Beauregard.

My mind had wandered and I'd clearly missed something. Everyone was looking at me, including my new friends, who were standing.

"What are you waiting for, Zoë?" Clarice said with a bit of a nervous laugh. "Don't be shy. Stand on up!"

She must have introduced Sai, Aaliyah, Jason and then

me, but I was the only one who had missed her cue. I stood up quickly, smiled, and waved, and the confused silence that filled the tent was replaced by scattered applause. From across the tent I could see the look of concern and worry on my mother's face. I felt my smile falter and quickly looked away. At that moment a photographer from the publicity team took a picture of the four of us.

That will be a keeper, I thought sarcastically.

ZOË WINTER DOESN'T LOOK THRILLED TO BE FILMING LATEST EPISODE OF *SCREAMERS*

"We've got some special activities and events planned throughout the week for you four," Clarice said, "including an on-set visit from author Jeremy Alexander Sinclair on Friday."

"What?" Jason said in shock. He looked like he needed to sit down. "No one told me I'd get to meet him!"

Clarice wrapped up her speech and Glenda reminded everyone that the first scene was being filmed bright and early at dawn. A lineup quickly formed at the sundae bar while other people began to stream out of the tent.

"I'm not going to be able to sleep tonight," Jason said. "I might not be able to sleep all week."

"Well, you should try," I cautioned. "All of us should. The first day on set is always exhausting."

"You don't have to tell me twice," Sai said. "I'm going

straight to sleep . . . after going over my lines one final time."

We wished each other good night and joined up with our parents, who showed us to our trailers. Mine was as sleek inside as it was outside. One side of the trailer extended out with the push of a button, making it surprisingly spacious. There were two sleeping areas with a double bed in one and a queen in the other, a sitting area with a TV, a kitchenette and a bathroom. I imagined the other kids were thrilled. Aaliyah had probably taken a million selfies already.

"How was your afternoon?" Mom asked.

"Tons of fun," I said, deciding to omit the fact we'd seen two old-timey ghosts and I suspected I'd seen a third. "Sai is as committed to acting as I thought when he auditioned, and Jason's really into . . . eating." I'd almost said ghost hunting, but that would have raised questions I didn't want to answer.

Mom cocked her eyebrow. "Oh. That's nice, I guess. And what about Aaliyah? Did you two hit it off?"

I thought about that and realized we hadn't connected as easily as I would've liked. "She's cool, but she seems a little distant." Was she having a similar conversation in her trailer with her dad? If so, what was she saying about me?

"How so?" Mom asked.

"We're just a little different, I guess. She's super focused on building a following online and having, like, fans."

Mom laughed a little at that.

"What's so funny?" I asked.

"You weren't so different a couple of years ago. You had stars for eyes too."

"And now I'd trade those stars in for a pair of those glasses with a fake nose and moustache so that no one would recognize me when I go out."

"I know," Mom said. "The price of fame." She eyed me suspiciously. "Are you having second thoughts about carrying on?"

I shook my head vigorously — maybe a little too vigorously. I hadn't told anyone about my secret desire to give it all up and live a more normal life. "No! Of course not."

"Well, I've decided to give you a break from homeschooling this week so you can focus on filming and having fun. Consider it your summer vacation."

"Seriously?"

Mom smiled and nodded.

"Thank you!" I gave her a tight hug, and for a moment I forgot all about ghosts.

Until later that night when I woke up to the sound of nails *tap-tap-tapping* on the window beside my head and saw a pair of eyes staring in at me.

CHAPTER
Ten

I clapped a hand over my mouth to stop myself from unleashing one of my world-famous screams.

"Zoë, it's me," said a voice, low and muffled by the windowpane.

I recognized that voice.

"Aaliyah?"

She nodded, her face slowly coming into focus as I stared out into the darkness.

I checked my bedside clock. "It's nearly midnight. What are you doing here?"

"I couldn't sleep and, well . . . can you come out here for a minute? I need to talk to you."

I rubbed my face and ran my fingers through my hair. "Yeah, sure. Give me a sec."

I grabbed my shoes and crept through the trailer. The door creaked as I opened it. I heard Mom roll over and snore loudly — luckily she was a deep sleeper. I slipped out into the night and closed the door gently behind me.

Aaliyah was there the instant I turned around.

I jumped, then raised my hands. "You have got to stop scaring me, okay?"

"Sorry," she said. "And thanks. I didn't know who else I could speak with."

"C'mon, let's move away from the trailers." We walked toward the entrance gate, locked for the night. The park's lights were still on, bathing everything in a warm yellow glow. It was beautiful. The problem was, we could still see the trailers from the gate. So if someone happened to wake up, we'd be spotted. "Here, give me a boost," I said.

Aaliyah smiled and nodded. She laced her fingers together and put out her hands palms up for me to step on, then I pulled myself over the gate. I reached through the bars and did the same to help her over.

"I didn't think you'd be the sneak-over-a-locked-gate-in-the-middle-of-the-night type, Zoë," Aaliyah said.

"First of all, we either go for a walk in here, in the light, or out there, in the dark woods. And second, you woke me up in the middle of the night, remember? I should be asleep and warm and cozy right now. So, do you care to tell me why you dragged me out here?"

"I'm scared," she said, jumping straight to the heart of the matter.

"Scared? Of what?" A cool breeze howled across our path

and made me shiver. I looked around to make sure we were still alone. "Wait . . . is it the ghosts?"

"Surprisingly, no," she said.

"Let's walk," I suggested. "It'll warm us up."

"But what if there are people here working through the night? What will we say?"

"We'll come up with an excuse," I said with a shrug. "It's called acting." I smiled, but Aaliyah didn't return it. If anything, what I'd said appeared to make her more upset.

We passed by a booth filled with Whac-a-Mole games and plush-toy prizes. String lights criss-crossed in the air, hanging down from the roof.

"So are you going to tell me what you're scared of? Or," I said, pointing at the light bulbs, "am I going to have to shine one of those directly into your face to make you talk?"

Aaliyah laughed, a good start. "The more time I spend with you, the more I believe you'd do that."

"Don't make me be the bad cop!"

"Okay, okay," she said, raising her hands in surrender. "Here's the deal. I'm scared of tomorrow."

"What about tomorrow?"

"All of it. I'm scared of Clarice, and the boys — especially Sai — and you."

"You're scared of me? Why?"

"You're such a good actor, Zoë, and Sai is so serious about it that he must be good too, and I'm afraid I . . . won't be."

First impressions were often wrong: I had thought Aaliyah was more interested in her social-media presence than acting, but maybe that was just what I saw on the surface. I of all people should have known better.

"You were selected because of how well you did on the screen test," I told her. "You have nothing to worry about."

She still didn't look convinced.

"Can I tell you a story?" I asked.

Aaliyah nodded.

Her nerves had reminded me what it had been like when I was just getting started. "I went to a lot of auditions before I landed my first *Screamers* episode," I began. "And I got almost as many rejections, but I was also booked to appear in a couple of commercials and I was an extra in a few different shows and movies. And then my agent scored me an audition for a small part in a musical."

"I love musicals," Aaliyah said.

"So do I, but there was one little problem: I couldn't sing. Not well, anyway. But my character only had to sing two lines and I had a couple of weeks to prepare. I took a few lessons and I practised singing every spare minute of every day. I got pretty good too, but I still felt like I was going to be sick when I walked onto the stage to audition. Butterflies in my stomach, sweaty palms, trembling knees — the works.

"A producer, the director and the music supervisor were

sitting in the theatre, and a woman joined me onstage and sat at a piano. The producer asked me something, but I was so nervous I didn't hear what she said. I froze. For a moment I considered running offstage, but then the director said something I'll never forget."

"What was it?" Aaliyah asked, hanging off my every word.

"He said, 'Don't be nervous. Acting and singing are expressions of our inner selves, and you strike me as a fun person. Just be yourself and have fun.'"

"And did you?" Aaliyah asked. "Have fun?"

"I did," I said, smiling at the memory. "Singing onstage in a real theatre was a thrill. They'd asked me to sing 'On My Own' from *Les Misérables* and I gave it my all. I let me be me. I had fun. I forgot some of the lyrics in the middle but I didn't let that stop me. I made some up and plowed on. I was filled to the brim with confidence as I bared my soul through song."

I paused in the telling of my story and took a deep breath, pre-emptively embarrassed by what came next.

"There was a moment of silence after I finished, and just as I was beginning to think I'd blown it, the music supervisor said, 'That was fantastic, Angela. Bravo!' I couldn't believe it! I was so excited that I started gushing, repeatedly thanking him and admitting that I'd never sung onstage before, how I'd been practising for days, how scared I'd been when I first walked out, how the director's kindness had helped me find my voice and how my name wasn't Angela but I didn't care that he'd gotten it wrong because he had said I was fantastic.

"There was another moment of silence, this one longer than the last. Finally the music supervisor said he knew my name was Zoë, that the pianist's name was Angela and that she was filling in for their regular pianist and it was the first time they'd heard her play.

"And then I ran offstage."

"Did you get the part?" Aaliyah asked sarcastically.

"Surprise, surprise, I did not. But the very next audition I had was for *Screamers*. I remembered the director's advice from the musical audition and the rest is history."

Aaliyah laughed. "That's pretty embarrassing."

"Yes, but I didn't let being scared make me give up on my dream of being a professional actor. Neither should you, if that's what you decide you want. Remember, be yourself and have fun."

"Thank you," Aaliyah said. "I don't feel as afraid anymore."

"That's good." What she said had reminded me of her screen test. "Speaking of being afraid, do you remember when we first met? You said something along the lines of ghost stories making you brave enough to face anything that might make you afraid in your day-to-day life."

She blushed to the tips of her ears and quickly looked away. "Oh, yeah, right. I realized almost immediately that I'd ripped you off. I had spent the days leading up to that reading and watching every interview of yours I could find online. Sorry."

"Don't worry about it!" I said, feeling a little flattered. "But you also said that shows like *Screamers* have helped you get through some dark times . . ."

I'd said it before I'd thought about it. I was a little concerned I'd brought up something too personal, but Aaliyah didn't shy away.

"It's true, they have," she said. "My mom died seven years ago. Cancer. It's just been me and my dad ever since and he works a lot, so I've spent a lot of time on my own. So what you said about ghost stories and being brave — I really took that to heart."

"I'm sorry, Aaliyah. My dad left when I was young," I blurted out, surprising myself. I'd never talked about that with anyone other than Mom. "He took everything we had, so my mom had to work two jobs while driving me to auditions all over the city after school. Like you, reading Goosebumps and watching shows like *Are You Afraid of the Dark?* on YouTube helped me get through those tough times. The monsters and ghosts and stuff made my life seem pretty great by comparison." I laughed darkly. "But now it's true what they say: truth is stranger than fiction."

She laughed with me. "You can say that again."

We had walked the whole time and reached the back of the park.

"I guess I thought that if I was famous, it might fill the void left by my mother's death," Aaliyah said. "For the rest of the week I'm going to cut back on selfies and posts, and focus on my performance. Who knows? Maybe I'll be the next Zoë Winter."

"Oh, trust me," I said. "Being me is highly overrated."

We laughed together, and I felt happier than I had in months.

"My advice is for you to be the next Aaliyah Hill," I said. "No one can do a better job at that than you. Are you ready to head back now?"

"Just about," Aaliyah said. She looked over my shoulder, then back to me. "But there's one more thing I want to do." Without warning she ran to The Laffin' Place.

"Aaliyah!" I shouted. "What do you think you're doing? We can't go in there in the middle of the night, alone."

She stopped in front of the door, turned back to me, and smiled widely. "Just kidding, Zoë," she said.

And then the door swung open, someone reached out from the inky darkness within, and Aaliyah disappeared inside with a Zoë Winter–calibre scream.

CHAPTER
Eleven

I charged straight through the clown's mouth and into the funhouse without hesitation, but there was no sign of Aaliyah or anyone else.

"Aaliyah!" I shouted.

"Ha ha, hee hee, ha ha ha, ho ho, haaa . . ." The laughter was full of static and hiss. Maybe it was an old recording, but I couldn't be sure. It felt like someone was taunting me.

It's Beauregard's ghost, I finally allowed myself to admit. *It was him watching you earlier in the day and he's the one who has Aaliyah.*

Hoping they were close, I ran, turned a corner, and screamed. I'd come face to face with . . . myself. It was a slim, warped mirror that made me look twice as tall and half as wide.

I hate funhouses, I thought as I continued through the halls. There was only one way to go, which was either a blessing or a curse. I didn't have to think — I just had to move quickly. But on the other hand, I felt a little like a lab rat being forced through a one-way maze, winding my way to the dead centre where I'd find Aaliyah too late, murdered, and I'd meet the same fate.

Don't think like that, I chided myself. *You've made too many* Screamers *episodes.*

Around another corner was a long tunnel that was rotating slowly. As soon as I ran into it, the tunnel sped up and rolled my feet out from under me. I landed hard on my back and had the wind knocked out of me. I groaned and gasped for air as the spinning tube rolled me over again and again. I crawled and scrambled forward as the tube continued to flip me over and the sides slammed against my legs, my arms, my chest and my head. I felt like a sack of bones trapped in a clothes dryer, but finally I reached the end and pulled myself out to solid ground.

My breath restored, I assessed the damage. I was sore all over but nothing too serious. Unsteadily I got to my feet. As tempting as it was to lay in a curled-up heap on the ground, I had to find Aaliyah.

The floor in the next hallway was made of panels that slid from side to side. I fell and banged my knee once or twice as I made my way through it. Compared to the rotating tunnel it was a walk in the park. But then, just as I was approaching the end, one of the last panels popped open, and out sprang a clown with glowing red eyes and a hideous laugh. A second clown with red eyes reached for me through a gap in the wall, and a third plunged down from a hiding place in the ceiling. It took me a moment to realize they were mechanical clowns on retractable arms, designed to pop out as soon as someone got close. I pushed away the fake clown in front of me and moved on.

I entered a room of mirrors. Like the one that had greeted me when I first entered The Laffin' Place, there were mirrors that made me look tall and thin, but there were also mirrors that made me look short and squat, mirrors that gave me an hourglass shape and mirrors that made me look closer or farther away than I was. There were two long mirrors facing one another that created a countless number of shrinking Zoës stretching to infinity. The last mirror in the room, framed and hung on the wall beside the exit, looked completely normal. I paused for a second or two, expecting something to happen. But nothing did.

As I started to turn away, another face — not my own — peered out at me from within the mirror. It was a girl, her eyes overlapping mine. It wasn't just any girl — it was Ghost Girl. Mist swirled around her shoulders.

Suddenly she shrieked and lunged out of the mirror, grabbing my neck. Her nails dug into my skin, and her ice-cold fingers sent freezing jolts of pain through my body like pulses of electricity. The mist flowed out of the mirror, released when she'd reached through the glass surface.

I couldn't breathe. I couldn't even scream. It felt like my eyes were about to pop out of my skull. I grabbed her hands but was unable to peel her fingers away.

The world started to dim. My vision started to fade. I had no energy left. I felt tired, so tired. If only I could sleep.

You can sleep, a voice said in my head. My own? It didn't matter. I could sleep — the voice had said so — and that was all that mattered.

I closed my eyes and drifted off. It felt like falling.

"You did this!" the girl from the mirror shouted in my face, waking me from the dark pit my mind had tumbled into. "This is all your fault! You and your friends are going to die!"

She let go of my throat. Her hands faded and disappeared, as did her arms, her shoulders, her face and her head. Her eyes remained for half a heartbeat until I blinked and they were gone.

I dropped to the ground and gasped for air. As the ice slowly melted from my veins and my body warmed up, my mind began to process what had just happened.

I rubbed my neck as I got back to my feet and was surprised to find that the skin on my neck wasn't sore. Fearful that Ghost Girl might return, I looked at my reflection once more. There were no bruises or scratches where she'd grabbed me. It was as if the attack had never happened. I shook it off and ran out of the room. There was no time to lose.

The next room, and the final one in the funhouse, judging by the EXIT sign above the door on the far side, looked like a small child's bedroom. There was a four-poster bed, a play table, small chairs and a bookcase. Every surface was covered in toys — specifically, clowns. There were stuffed clowns, plastic clowns and antique porcelain clowns. Famous clowns like Ronald McDonald, Krusty the Clown and The Joker. There were also other dolls and figurines dressed to resemble clowns. I spotted Sadie Sees, a doll I'd had when I was a kid, just like most girls my age. Her face had been painted white, and her nose and mouth were smeared red. I pictured her eyes moving left to right the way they used to, which had always creeped me out a little, and her mouth opening to utter one of her equally creepy catchphrases: "Wouldn't it be fun if you were a doll like me?"

The largest clown doll — it was the same size as me — was lying on the bed as if in a deep sleep. There was no sign of Aaliyah or Beauregard, but then the clown on the bed shifted.

My heart leapt into my throat and I fought back tears. What fresh horror was this?

The clown doll's chest rose and fell. It was alive. It shifted again, groaned, then sat up slowly.

I noticed a black elastic string stretched around the back of its head. It wasn't a doll — it was a person wearing a cheap plastic clown mask. As soon as I realized that, a hand reached up and removed the mask, revealing a familiar face.

"Aaliyah!" I shouted as I ran to her, wrapping my arms around her in relief.

"I think I fell asleep," she said groggily. "Or passed out. What happened?" Her eyes suddenly went wide with fear and she pointed a trembling finger over my shoulder.

I turned around.

Beauregard was standing between us and the bookcase full of toy clowns.

"Boo!" he jeered.

CHAPTER
Twelve

I screamed and so did Aaliyah. Beauregard screamed in return. For a brief, confusing moment, I thought we had somehow frightened him, but then as he started to laugh I realized he'd been mocking us.

It began as a deep, guttural sound that seemed to reverberate through the air before rising to a high-pitched squeal of delight. Beauregard's wide frilly collar shook, and he held his belly like a sick, demented version of Santa Claus. He wore the same black-and-white outfit we'd seen on his cut-out, and his makeup was identical too: white face paint, big red lips, a round red nose, thin black lines over his eyes and three tufts of red hair sticking out of his skull that made him look like he'd given himself a haircut with a pair of rusty hedge shears.

I looked to the door with the red EXIT sign, planning our escape. If we ran fast enough, maybe we could make it out before he reached us. *Go,* I thought. *Run!* But my legs wouldn't budge and Aaliyah also appeared to be frozen with fear.

Beauregard's laughter wound down, ending with a brief choking sound. He clapped three times.

"Oh boy," he said. "I sure do love to laugh." He laughed one, two, three more times, then wiped at the corner of his eye.

A bead of sweat ran down my face, from forehead to chin, and dripped to the floor.

There was a long, drawn-out pause, a period of silence that felt like an eternity.

"Don't you love to laugh?" Beauregard asked. He took a few steps toward us. His clown shoes slapped the ground, and the floorboards creaked beneath them. "Or do you prefer to cry?"

It was too much for me. Too much to handle, and far too much to believe. A tear formed in the corner of my eye, clung to my eyelashes for a second, then broke free.

Beauregard's eyes widened and his smile grew impossibly large. My fear made him laugh again, this time louder than before, a hooting sound that cut through me like a knife.

"You do love to cry," he exclaimed with joy. "You do, you do, you do. I can't tell you how happy that makes me." He smiled more widely than humanly possible, and it wasn't just an effect of his painted red lips. His actual lips stretched up and to the sides of his face, practically all the way to his earlobes, baring his large teeth and blood-red gums.

"What do you want with us?" I blurted out.

"What do I want with you?" Beauregard asked. "Why, my dear girl, I want the same thing I've always wanted with everyone — an audience. I want to perform. I want to entertain. I want to make you . . . laugh." He ran his hand up his face, revealing a broad smile. "And if I can't make you laugh, I'll make you cry." He slowly ran his hand back down, revealing a frown. "Or better yet, I'll make you die." Beauregard ran a finger across his throat and then erupted into hysterics, hooting and hollering between laughs and giggles. He bent over and slapped his knee, his face pointed at the floor.

I saw our opportunity, and this time I didn't hesitate to seize it. There probably wouldn't be another.

"Quick, Aaliyah," I said quietly but urgently. "Run!"

I grabbed her hand and sprinted as fast as I could across the room.

Beauregard's laughter stopped abruptly. He roared in anger and lunged for us with bony fingers painted white.

I pushed the crash bar and slammed my shoulder into the door. It swung open and Aaliyah and I tumbled out and ran as fast as we could. I only looked back once, when we'd run far enough for me to build a little courage to do so. Beauregard was standing outside The Laffin' Place, in the same spot I'd seen him that afternoon, his chest and shoulders heaving. At first I couldn't tell if he was laughing or crying. It sounded like he was doing both at the same time.

"Who's excited to meet our clown?" Glenda asked.

Her smile faltered when no one answered. Sai was pacing around our breakfast table, a largely ignored plate of bacon and eggs where he'd sat, muttering his dialogue for our first scene of the day. Jason's nose was in a Haunted Coasts book. And although we hadn't spoken a word of what had happened to us the night before, Aaliyah and I exchanged a knowing, sickened look at the thought of spending any more time with clowns.

"Yeesh, tough crowd," Glenda said. I felt a little bad for her. Usually the members of the cast — especially the young actors — were pumped to see the episode's villain for the first time. Glenda shrugged and called with little enthusiasm or fanfare, "All right, Gary, c'mon out."

A man in a colourful outfit and a rubber clown mask jumped into the tent, gloved hands raised like claws, and roared. The sound was more like that of a small bear in search of honey than a killer clown out for blood. He dropped his arms, stood up straight, and pulled off the mask.

"Hi, everyone," he said. "I'm Gary. I'm playing Beauregard."

"You don't say," Jason said dryly, briefly looking up from his book.

Now I felt a little bad for Glenda *and* Gary. "Nice to meet you, Gary. I'm Zoë."

The others didn't introduce themselves so I took over. "This is Jason — he loves ghosts more than anyone I know, and that's saying something when you work on a show like *Screamers*. Sai over there is a super-dedicated actor, as you can tell by the fact that he's too busy rehearsing dialogue he's already had memorized for weeks to eat. And Aaliyah . . ." I'd been about to say that Aaliyah was my new best friend, but I didn't want to embarrass her or scare her off. Instead I said, "She's going to be a star one day."

"Nice to meet you all," Gary said. "I know I look scary in this costume, but I promise I'm not as scary as a killer ghost clown in real life."

I laughed far too loudly, partly due to how close Gary's comment had hit home and partly out of the absurdity of what we were secretly living through. Gary raised his eyebrow and looked like he was wondering if I was okay. Aaliyah shook her head and elbowed me to stop.

"That's funny," I said, trying to explain why I had reacted the way I had. "Can you imagine if there actually were killer ghost clowns in real life? Pennyland would be the last place I'd want to be."

Gary nodded and said, "Yeah, I guess." He was probably

still wondering if there was something wrong with me, but fortunately he dropped it and we moved on.

The first scene to be filmed was straightforward and would serve as the opening shot of the episode. The four of us had to enter through the main gates, talking about all the things we wanted to do during our visit to the amusement park. My character, Chloe — and the viewer, for that matter — didn't know yet that Pennyland was a figment of my imagination and that my three "friends" and I were actually being admitted to a psychiatric hospital. At the end of the scene, after we had entered the park, the camera would keep rolling for a beat before Beauregard — played by the one and only Gary — crept into frame laughing maniacally. Or maybe just growling like a hungry bear . . . I wasn't sure what sort of energy Gary was planning on bringing to his performance.

As we left the tent and approached the front gate, I squeezed Aaliyah's elbow and slowed my pace. She frowned but slowed down with me. Once there was enough distance between us and the others, I whispered, "You okay?"

Aaliyah shook her head. "I don't know. You?"

"I don't know," I answered honestly.

"Did that really happen last night?"

"Unfortunately."

"I was afraid of that." Aaliyah rubbed her eyes. "I'm so tired. I feel like a zombie. I think I had conversations with, like, five different people on my way to breakfast this morning but the details are all just gone." She put her hand to her head and made a mind-blown gesture.

"I'm wiped too." I'd tossed and turned for most of the night, partly out of fear, and partly from wondering what I should do. "Listen, we can tell our parents or someone from the production about it if you want."

"If we say something," Aaliyah said, "who would believe us? And even if they did believe us, what would they do? Perform an exorcism? Call the Ghostbusters? Bring in Jeremy Sinclair to write a book about it?"

Glenda looked back over her shoulder at us and raised an eyebrow.

"I know what you're saying," I said. "It might be best to keep it down."

There was a large camera on a dolly track at the park entrance. Crew members were buzzing about as they set up equipment. Clarice was talking to the assistant director when she saw us.

"There they are!" she called, approaching us with a wide smile. "The stars of the show. Did everyone get a good night's sleep?"

All four of us nodded, but Aaliyah and I exchanged another look — it was becoming our thing.

"Glad to hear it," Clarice said. "For this opening shot I want you all to act so excited that I get excited, okay?"

"Got it," I said, glancing at the others. Aaliyah looked tired, Jason looked remarkably calm and Sai looked incredibly focused. *I hope this goes well*, I thought as we took our places. The camera operator double-checked the framing of the shot. The boom operator extended a microphone on a pole over our heads. And Clarice sat in her director's chair behind a playback monitor.

"Places, everyone," she said. "Remember, kids, you're excited to be here and have no idea there's a ghost clown lurking in the shadows, plotting your demise. And . . . action!"

"This is going to be so much fun, you guys!" I said, all sunshine and bubbles as we walked toward Pennyland's gate with our arms linked. "I haven't been to an amusement park in years!"

"I'm going to ride the Ferris wheel!" Aaliyah said.

"I'm going to ride the roller coaster!" Jason said.

"I'm going to eat so much popcorn that I puke," Sai said. Although the dialogue wasn't exactly Shakespeare, I had to hand it to Sai. He really embodied the character and sold me on his motivation. I truly believed he was going to eat so much popcorn that he'd puke. The boy could act.

"Let's not forget the circus tent, guys," I added. "I've always loved clowns." Considering what had happened in The Laffin' Place, I now found my dialogue to be a little unsettling. "Think there'll be a clown here in Pennyland?"

"If there's not, I'm going to ask for my money back, and

I'm not clowning around," Sai proclaimed with mock severity.

He was good. Really good.

The four of us laughed, placed some money on the counter of one of the ticket booths, and walked off-screen.

Gary stepped into frame holding a bloody knife (*perhaps a little over-the-top*, I thought from where I watched) and threw his head back with laughter. He sounded more like The Joker and less like Winnie the Pooh, which was a relief.

"And cut!" Clarice said. "Excellent work, everybody. I think we got it in one take." She looked at Aaliyah, Jason and Sai. "You three are officially television stars. Take a break. We'll call you when we're ready for the next scene."

The guys high-fived and Aaliyah and I hugged. She whipped out her phone, then frowned and shoved it back in her pocket.

I had a feeling I knew what she was thinking. "I know what you said last night in the park, but why don't you take a few pictures?" I said. "This is a nice moment. It would be good to capture it."

She smiled and grabbed her phone again, and the four of us took a series of group selfies in front of the Pennyland sign at the entrance. Gary photobombed the last one wearing his clown mask, and I decided he was okay. Aaliyah posted one of the pics to Instagram, tagged Jason, Sai and me, and wrote:

just hangin with my 3 new friends. you probably recognize 1 of them but the other 2 are going to be #stars soon too! #screamers #acting #whatismylife

Three new friends. I felt like I was walking on air.

"Wait a minute," Sai said, looking at me with a frown. "Did you say you were in the park last night?"

Jason perked up. "You didn't go hunting for ghosts without me, did you?"

I looked around at all the crew members milling about.

"Let's go find a quiet spot to talk," I said.

CHAPTER
Thirteen

The wind rustled through the low-hanging leaves of the willow tree we sat beneath. The buzz from filming had disappeared, replaced by the same low-level dread I'd felt for much of the previous day.

Aaliyah and I told the boys everything that had happened in The Laffin' Place. All things considered, they took it pretty well.

"I feel like I'm going to throw up," Sai said.

"Me too," Jason said. "I can't believe they didn't invite me to tag along."

"We're very different people," Sai told Jason.

Jason nodded and rested his chin on his forearms on top of his bent knees.

I patted Jason's shoulder sympathetically. He looked like a sad puppy sitting alone in the rain. "There, there, buddy. We'll take you with us next time."

"Promise?"

"Promise."

He smiled, but Sai looked concerned. "Let me get this straight. A killer ghost clown threatened to murder you in a nightmarish funhouse and you *want to go back?*"

"Well, yeah," I said. "If we're not going to tell anyone about what happened to us, we need to take matters into our own hands. We need to find out more about Beauregard so we can figure out how to get rid of him. Not only to keep us safe, but to protect anyone else who visits this park when it reopens."

Sai considered this for a moment, then nodded and said, "I hate to admit it, but you have a point."

"The park . . . That reminds me," Aaliyah said with a snap of her fingers. "I think Harriett was one of the five people who talked to me this morning."

Sai looked to Jason and mouthed, "Five people?"

Jason mouthed, "Harriett?" in response.

Sai sighed and mouthed, "Beth," to which Jason mouthed, "Ah," but then immediately looked more confused than ever.

Aaliyah frowned and thought a little harder. "She gave me something and told me to show it to my friends." She reached into her back pocket and unfolded a piece of paper.

"What is that?" Jason said.

We crowded in close and read over Aaliyah's shoulder.

It was a photocopy of a newspaper article dated October 2, 1937.

RECENTLY FIRED PENNYLAND CLOWN BEAUREGARD DIES DURING HOSTAGE SITUATION IN TRAGIC END TO NOTABLE CAREER

WINNIPEG—Pennyland's once beloved clown, Beauregard, who had given nightly performances at the amusement park for much of the past thirteen years before being fired in September, has died while giving an unsanctioned performance to an audience held against their will. Allegedly, Beauregard, whose real name is Lon Beaumont, locked a group of four minors in Pennyland's circus tent after the amusement park closed last night, and gave an odd, desperate performance that terrified his hostages. Beaumont died when he fell from an elevated trapeze platform.

This is the latest in a recent string of odd incidents involving Beaumont. After Pennyland closed for the winter season in November of last year, Beaumont was informed that he would no longer perform in the circus show, but instead would be a street performer wandering throughout the park. Pennyland officials cite a lack of customer satisfaction and interest in Beaumont's performance as the main reason for his removal from the circus show and his eventual firing last month. But many guests to the park have also reported that throughout the year Beaumont's behaviour had been growing increasingly erratic, even aggressive. He is said to have uttered profanities and lunged at a group of teenagers who mocked him shortly before he was fired.

"He was never what I'd call sociable," said Frank Cottrell, a trapeze artist in the Pennyland circus troupe who had known Beaumont for years. "But the clown gave a good show, I'll give him that, and it didn't matter that he wasn't friendly behind the scenes. The audience loved him!"

Other people who worked with Beaumont were less diplomatic.

"He was creepy," said Isabella Jardir, a Pennyland tightrope walker. "We all had to call him Beauregard, even when we were on break. I knew nothing about him. He stayed in his clown costume and makeup all day and night."

For years Beauregard and the circus show were highlights among Pennyland guests, and the show reached capacity nearly every night. People enjoyed his mix of slapstick comedy and genuine pathos. But audiences' tastes have changed in recent years, and the addition of the park's two towering thrill rides, The Big Thrill and Death Deflyer, in 1933 and 1935 respectively, attracted guests who sought out a more hair-raising form of entertainment.

However, The Big Thrill has still not reopened since the tragic accident on May 29 that claimed the lives of a sixteen-year-old girl and a seventeen-year-old boy. The young couple from Winnipeg died when their basket overturned and they fell nearly ten metres to the ground below. Authorities suspected foul play, as a malfunction on Death Deflyer on the same day nearly resulted in a separate accident. All Pennyland employees, including Beaumont, were questioned, but the ongoing investigation has not yet resulted in any charges.

Although the four minors Beaumont took hostage on Friday were not available for comment, it is reported that they are upset but sustained no injuries. According to authorities, Beaumont performed many traditional circus roles during his performance, which is what led to his fall from the trapeze platform. He threatened his hostages if they closed their eyes or looked away, demanding they watch his final show, and he repeatedly shouted, "If I can't make you laugh, I'll make you cry!"

Pennyland is currently closed while the investigation is ongoing, and one must wonder if the amusement park will be able to reopen or if it will be shuttered for the remainder of the season.

"Yeesh," Sai said. "That's a lot to unpack."

"It all lines up!" Jason said excitedly. "Beauregard was demoted from the circus show at the end of one season, and at the start of the very next season there were suspicious accidents involving The Big Thrill and Death Deflyer. The two people who died on The Big Thrill were both teenagers. People weren't interested in Beauregard's street performance and teens taunted him, so near the end of that season he snapped and forced some other teens to watch him perform in the tent — he even called it his final show. Seems pretty obvious that the two ghosts we've seen are the kids who died on the Ferris wheel, and that Beauregard was responsible for the accident that killed them. He clearly has it out for kids . . . like us." He pointed to the newspaper article in Aaliyah's hands. "Can I have that?"

"Sure, knock yourself out," Aaliyah said, handing Jason the clipping. She looked a little relieved to be rid of it, like it was contaminated or something.

My mind was racing, putting the pieces together. "Jason, what was it you said yesterday? Something about the past and ghosts moving on?"

"All ghosts are in the past," he said, "because they can't move on."

"Right," I said with a nod. "Beauregard — Lon Beaumont — was a weird guy and he was obsessed with his clown persona. All he wanted to do was perform, and when Pennyland took that away from him, he did horrendous things . . . but he didn't get to complete his final show."

"Are you saying what I think you're saying?" Sai asked.

"I'm saying that I think he might move on if he gets to perform his final, *final* show."

"He's a ghost," Aaliyah said. "He's had, like, more than eighty years to perform a final show. So why is he still here?"

"What does every performer need?" I asked.

"Professional headshots?" Jason joked. "The ability to speak in a dozen different accents? A part-time job as a waiter?"

"An audience," Sai said.

"Bingo," I said, pointing at Sai. "That's why Beauregard hasn't moved on. He needs an audience." I looked from Sai to Aaliyah to Jason — the first two looked less than thrilled, while the third looked more excited than I'd ever seen him. "He needs us."

Fourteen

"**A**ction!"

The rest of the morning and afternoon was spent filming, but the one-take wonder from the morning was a one-time wonder itself.

"Cut!"

Filming took much longer than usual, with anywhere from fifteen to twenty takes per shot.

"Action!"

I even managed to mess up a scene where all I had to do was yell, "Look out!" while pulling Aaliyah out of the way of a spray of acid from Beauregard's lapel flower. Don't ask me how a ghost would manage to fill a flower with acid.

We were filming in front of The Laffin' Place, and I couldn't concentrate on my performance. I kept looking over my shoulder, checking to make sure Beauregard — the real Beauregard, not Gary — didn't float through the walls. And every time I closed my eyes to focus, all I saw was the creepy clown room with all the dolls.

Just as I was beginning to worry that Clarice was going to lose her voice from yelling "Action!" and "Cut!" so many times, my mind went completely blank during the middle of the scene. Everyone stared at me with a mixture of anticipation, embarrassment and compassion. I knew I was supposed to say something, but I had no idea what my next line was.

"Cut!" Clarice stood up from her chair and looked around at the crew. "Everyone take five."

The set emptied as I dropped my character's timid demeanour and got to my feet. After so many silly mistakes I had trouble meeting Clarice's eyes.

Aaliyah, Sai and Jason crossed the path and huddled together near a popcorn cart, casting pitying glances my way.

"I'm really sorry, Clarice," I said. I put a hand to my forehead, pretending to check my temperature. "I don't know what's wrong with me today. I never have this much trouble remembering my lines. You know that."

"I do." Clarice smiled sympathetically. "So what's the problem?"

I shook my head, trying to think what to say. "I'm not sure . . . I ate the fish at lunch even though it smelled a little extra fishy. Maybe I have food poisoning?"

"You don't look sick," Clarice said. "Have you thrown up since you ate?"

"No."

"Then it's probably not food poisoning." When I sighed, Clarice quickly added, "That's good news! A bout of food poisoning would lay you up for a day or two and put the production behind schedule. And look, it's no big deal. Everyone has off days. And sometimes there's no reason why."

"I guess," I said, thinking about the very good reason why I was having an "off day."

Clarice looked at her watch. "It's almost dinnertime and I think we got most of what we need. We should be able to cobble together sections of each take to make this scene work. Let's take a break and move on. Sound good?"

"Yeah, sounds good." Clarice was smiling at me like she was hiding something. "What's up?" I asked her.

She looked like she was about to explode with anticipation. "I was going to save this surprise announcement for dinnertime, but what the heck! I'm no good with secrets." She turned and waved the others over. "Aaliyah! Jason! Sai! Come over here!"

Once they'd joined us, Clarice said, "I've got great news: I spoke with Pennyland's management this afternoon and they informed me that Death Deflyer and The Big Thrill have passed inspection. You four get to be the first kids in the country to ride them since they've been renovated!"

And the news got even "better." Glenda was able to re-arrange the shooting schedule so that our evening was free.

The rest of the afternoon vanished in the blink of an eye. Before I had time to think too much about the night ahead, I was meeting up with the others in front of The Big Thrill as the sun set in the distance.

"Funny how twenty-four hours can completely change your point of view," Aaliyah said. "Yesterday I was excited to test some of the rides, and now I'm terrified."

Jason nodded. "After what happened to you last night and what we learned about Beauregard, I'm not exactly thrilled by the thought anymore either."

Jason seemed to be a little braver than the rest of us, so what he said spoke volumes.

"Do you think if I close my eyes and think happy thoughts I can keep my acrophobia in check?" Sai asked.

"You have a fear of acrobats?" Jason asked.

"What? No. Acrophobia is the fear of heights."

"That makes more sense," Jason said matter-of-factly.

"Maybe we're all overreacting," I offered. "I'm sure the rides are completely safe, not to mention fun. And let's not forget that Beauregard tampered with the rides ages ago in the 1930s — Death Deflyer and The Big Thrill have been repaired and upgraded since then. Plus, the clown wasn't dead back then! Even if a ghost could still do what he did when he was alive, rides have all kinds of new safety measures and backup systems."

"She's right!" someone behind us said loudly, making me jump.

"Harriett!" Jason said in shock.

Sai raised a finger and opened his mouth to correct Jason, then changed course. "Huh. You got it right this time."

"The odds are fifty-fifty," Jason conceded, "so I was bound to be right eventually."

"Nothing will go wrong on these rides," Harriett said. "Trust me."

I silenced the voice in the back of my head that spoke up to remind me that Harriett was so new at Pennyland she didn't even have a uniform with her own name on it. Harriett might be new at this park, but she was still in charge of the rides. If she said they were safe, they must be.

So why did I still have a flutter of butterflies in my stomach?

"But did I hear you right?" Harriett said. "Did you say something about a ghost messing with the rides?"

"What?" I said with a smile and what I hoped sounded like a carefree laugh. "No, of course not. I don't know *anything* about ghosts."

"You star in a show all about ghosts," Harriett pointed out.

I snapped my fingers. "Yes! That's what we were talking

about. The ghost in the episode we're filming."

"All right," Harriett said slowly, leading me to believe she hadn't fully bought into my lie but wasn't going to pursue the matter any further . . . or maybe she just thought I was a little weird. "Did you read the article I gave Aaliyah this morning?"

"We sure did!" Jason said excitedly.

"Good," Harriett said. "I found it pinned to a bulletin board in the staff room, sticking out from behind some posters. Looked like it'd been there a long time, so I figured no one's going to miss it. And since you were asking so many questions yesterday I knew you'd be interested." She checked her watch and said, "Oh! Check this out! In three, two, one . . ."

With a sharp crack of electricity, all the lights turned on at once. Carnival music played from speakers on poles. A moment later an empty Death Deflyer train sped along the rickety wooden track. The Big Thrill's wheel began moving slowly. Recorded laughter — the same menacing sound I'd heard the night before — drifted out from The Laffin' Place. And spotlights flooded the sky above the circus tent.

Sitting in the glow of a million twinkling lights, we held a collective breath. The sight all around us gave me the chills. But in a good way.

"Isn't she beautiful?" Harriett asked.

I didn't know if she was referring to a particular ride

or building, or the entire park, but I would've agreed with Harriett either way.

"Good evening, everyone," Clarice said as she approached. "How incredible is this place at night with all the lights on and the rides in motion? The crew is just setting up a few things and then we'll be ready to start shooting."

"You mean, we have to film tonight? We can't go on the rides after all?"

Clarice laughed. "Lucky for you, no. We're going to film some B-roll — shots of the rides, the games, the snacks and, most importantly, people enjoying the park. Our extras should be arriving any minute, but I told the crew not to bug the four of you on your night off so that you get to enjoy the rides in peace."

"More like in *pieces*," Jason muttered.

"What was that?" Clarice asked.

"Nothing!" he said, his cheeks reddening.

"Well, off you go!" Clarice said.

"I recommend you go on Death Deflyer first," Harriett said. "That way you can get your heart rate under control on The Big Thrill." She tried to suppress a laugh — some sort of private joke — that made it impossible to trust what she'd said.

Jason and Sai exchanged looks with me and Aaliyah. Looks that seemed to say, *Are we really doing this?* I nodded.

"Thanks for the tip, Harriett," I said. "What do you all say?"

No one argued, but I could tell they weren't thrilled.

We'll be fine, I reassured myself. But even my internal voice had a hint of desperation and doubt.

We started toward Death Deflyer and, like four moths trapped in the world's largest, brightest, most dangerous flame, prepared for the ride of our lives.

CHAPTER
Fifteen

Within fifteen minutes, Pennyland came screaming to life.

So far, I had only seen Pennyland employees and *Screamers* crew members in the park, but it was suddenly filled with people. Two busloads of extras streamed into the area where filming was set to take place. Some remained in their regular street clothes to portray guests, and others were given Pennyland uniforms and assigned to different attractions to pretend to be working there. Children ran and squealed with joy as laughing parents chased after them, groups of teenagers criss-crossed from one attraction to another and young couples walked hand in hand.

Pennyland staff members called out to passersby, encouraging them to play their games. "Step right up and I'll guess your weight and age!" and "Test your skill. See if your aim is true. A prize in every balloon!"

We looked around in amazement. The park had gone

from being quiet and lifeless to being full of excitement and wonder. For the first time in a long time I felt like a regular kid visiting an amusement park with her friends, not an actress on a television set who was constantly looking over her shoulder for ghosts. It felt nice. Really nice.

Behind us The Big Thrill revolved hypnotically, and in front of us a Death Deflyer train sped past with a *clickety-clack, clickety-clack*, bringing me back to reality.

A line of extras had formed to board Death Deflyer. We paused before joining it.

"Listen," I said, my voice cracking and my palms sweaty. "We can bail. No one is forcing us to go on any of these rides."

Aaliyah and Jason seemed to be considering my offer when Sai raised his hands and stormed forward. "This is ridiculous. It's just a ride!" He joined the line without even waiting to see if we'd follow him.

There was a moment of stunned silence among us before Jason said, "If the guy with aerophobia is going, then I'm going too."

"Acrophobia," Aaliyah said. "But if the ride breaks down and one of the trains sails off the track, I'm sure we'll all develop a case of aerophobia as well."

The three of us quickly joined Sai, who already looked like he was having second thoughts.

"It's just a ride," he repeated a few times quietly to

himself. "A really, really, really tall ride."

"You got this, buddy," Jason said, patting Sai on the back.

"Yeah," Aaliyah said. She looked up at the peak of the wooden track. "It will be . . . fun."

"And we'll all be together," I added, hoping that would be as big a selling feature for the others as it was for me.

The line wasn't very long and we reached the loading platform pretty quick, which was a good thing. It gave us less time to think about the ride and freak out more than any of us already had. We were directed by one of the ride operators to sit in the front two rows. Sai was pale and starting to sweat, so I linked arms with Aaliyah and guided us to the front row, allowing Sai and Jason to sit behind us. That way we wouldn't be behind Sai if he was sick on the ride.

We buckled our seat belts and pulled down on the lap bar before the operator checked everything was securely fastened. And then, with a thumbs-up from another operator in the control booth, our train started forward.

"This was a mistake," Sai said.

"Some of the best times I've ever had started out as mistakes," Jason said with a shaky voice that made me think he was trying to cover his nerves with a little humour.

Aaliyah had closed her eyes and was digging her nails into the padding on our lap bar.

And me? My fear completely evaporated the moment we

began to climb the first hill. I hadn't felt this happy since I'd first been offered a role in *Screamers*. I raised my arms in the air and screamed — with joy, not fear — as we crested the peak of the hill and began our rapid and steep descent. Then in a flash we quickly started up the second hill and my screams turned to laughter.

And I wasn't alone. Aaliyah had opened her eyes and was laughing beside me, and I could hear the boys laughing behind us too. Our train dipped and dived and took a few tight turns, and all four of us cheered and clapped when we returned to the loading platform a little less than three minutes after the ride had started.

"That was awesome!" Jason said as we exited the ride.

"I loved every moment," Aaliyah said.

"You survived, Sai," I said with a smile.

"It didn't cure my fear of heights," he said, "but it didn't kill me either. Even though no one paid me a million bucks to ride it, I'll take not dying as a win."

"Want to ride it again?" I asked.

He held up a hand. "Nah. I'm good for, like, a year or ten."

We laughed and made our way through the park. A family entered The Laffin' Place as we neared it, and seeing that it was open to guests made me stop short. I had no desire to go back in, but I knew Jason would want to. Sure enough, he started to cross the pathway toward the building without a word, on cruise control.

Aaliyah gave me a nervous look, clearly concerned we'd have to go back inside. What we'd been through — her especially — the night before would take some time to get past, so I offered her a reassuring smile and called to Jason.

"Hey, Jason! How about we skip The Laffin' Place for now and you can come back later if you want?"

His face fell. "But, but, but . . . *ghosts*."

An idea hit me. "What about we go on The Big Thrill? Odds are pretty good we'll find some ghosts there, right?"

An elderly couple passing by raised their eyebrows at us and quickly hurried on.

"Just practising some dialogue," I called after them.

Jason's expression brightened. "Sounds good," he said.

We walked for a few more minutes until we arrived at The Big Thrill.

"Are you going to be okay with this ride?" Jason asked Sai.

"After not fainting or puking on Death Deflyer," Sai said, "I feel like I'll be fine on this Ferris wheel."

"It goes a lot higher than Death Deflyer," Aaliyah said.

Sai groaned as if suddenly remembering that.

"But it's so much slower," Aaliyah added reassuringly. "And after surviving the coaster, you're a ride warrior now!"

Sai groaned again, but the sound was slightly more up-beat and optimistic.

Each cabin of The Big Thrill seated two people. I approached the loading platform with Aaliyah, the boys right behind us. The attendant, a young man in a park uniform, tipped his hat as he held the cabin door open. "Enjoy your ride, ladies," he said. Aaliyah and I sat side by side and buckled up. He checked that our seat belts were securely fastened and shut the door — *CLANG!* — sealing us in.

"Hey, are you okay?" Aaliyah whispered.

"Sure," I said. "It's just a Ferris wheel."

"No, not that," Aaliyah said quietly. "Filming today seemed a little . . . difficult."

"I guess I had a bad day. It happens all the time, and that's even when we're not filming in an actual haunted location. Turns out, it's a little distracting."

Aaliyah laughed at that and looked relieved. "Can I tell you a story?"

I nodded, curious. Out of the corner of my eye I spotted the boys getting into the cabin behind us.

"Once upon a time I was scared because I felt inferior to this amazing actress I was working with on a show. You might have heard of it: It's called *Screamers?*"

I laughed and said, "Um, yes. That name does ring a bell."

"Well, I told that actress how I was feeling, and she shared some advice that had been given to her. She told me that acting is an expression of our inner selves and I should remember to have fun. I took that to heart and had a ton of fun filming my first few scenes."

"This actress," I said. "She sounds amazing."

"Oh, she is," Aaliyah said. "I'm lucky to have her as a friend. But that advice can be applied to real life too. I'm always going to remember to have fun no matter what I'm doing. And so should you."

It was silly, but my eyes began to water and I nearly started to cry. What Aaliyah had said really hit home. I wrapped my arms around her tightly. "Thank you."

"Thank *you*," she said. We separated and looked around. "Isn't this amazing? We have an entire amusement park practically to ourselves!"

"I know, right? Here's to having fun with new friends!"

"Hear, hear!"

Our cabin rocketed into the air much faster than I had anticipated. My stomach lurched, a ticklish and slightly nauseating sensation. Aaliyah and I laughed, and I heard the boys cheering in their cabin as we soared up high.

The view from the top of the wheel was breathtaking. We could see the entire amusement park, and from our height everyone below looked like insects. In the distance I caught sight of a fast-moving Death Deflyer train packed with extras. The lineups at the food booths were short and I decided I'd treat my friends to whatever they wanted once we got off The Big Thrill. And the circus tent seemed to glow under the thousands of lights in the park.

"This is incredible!" I shouted, putting my arm around Aaliyah's shoulders.

"Amazing!" Aaliyah said, taking in the sights with a childlike look of wonder on her face.

The wind whipped my hair around and made tears stream down my cheeks.

You do love to cry. You do, you do, you do.

It was Beauregard's voice speaking softly in my head. I looked back at the boys. Nothing seemed amiss. Clearly the events from the night before were still weighing on me. Unfortunately they probably would for a long time to come.

As I turned to face forward, Ghost Girl materialized between me and Aaliyah, her mouth hanging open as she stared straight ahead with her dead eyes. Mist rose around her and encircled all of us.

"You're both as good as dead," Ghost Girl said. She turned her head slowly to face me. Blood soaked through her hair and ran down her face. "Like me."

CHAPTER
Sixteen

There was no escape. We were at the peak of the Ferris wheel, trapped forty metres in the air with a ghost. My mind raced, trying to think of some way off the ride and out of this nightmare. The only thing I could think to do was to yell and scream at everyone below to let us off, but it would still take a while for us to return to the ground.

Our cabin lurched with a loud metallic grating sound.

Aaliyah and I were jostled in our seats and looked at each other with heightened concern.

"This is how I died," Ghost Girl said.

It felt like something had come loose in the rigging that connected our cabin to the outer edge of the wheel. My fear of Ghost Girl was replaced by the fear of falling to my death.

"Where did she come from?" Sai yelled from behind us.

Before I could answer, we started to descend and our cabin lurched again, this time even more violently. Aaliyah and I exchanged another look and we both checked to make sure our seat belts were tightly fastened.

"When our cabin came loose and hit the ground," Ghost Girl said, "I shot forward and slammed my head into these bars." She reached out her arm and traced her pale fingers along the cage in front of us. "At least it was over in a flash. I didn't feel a thing. Hopefully you won't either."

Was Ghost Girl causing this? Had she tampered with the ride? If so, why did she want to kill me and Aaliyah? Jealousy of the living? Misery loves company? Was she doing Beauregard's bidding?

"Nicholas has never forgiven me," Ghost Girl said. "I was the one who wanted to ride The Big Thrill. Like your friend, he was afraid of heights."

I briefly imagined Sai's ghost haunting mine for our entire afterlives, angry that we'd talked him into going on the thrill rides. I turned around, noticing their cabin was also bounding back and forth. "Hang on tight!" I said. It probably wouldn't save us, but I didn't want to admit there was nothing we could do to protect ourselves and save our lives. Sai and Jason both looked terrified as they grabbed on to the metal bars of their cabin.

I heard a metallic *snap* and our cabin rocked forward a third time. We rocketed backwards toward the middle of the Ferris wheel. The cabin came to an abrupt stop when it reached the centre, and Aaliyah and I both screamed.

Before we could say or do anything else, our cabin zipped

back to its original position at the outer rim of the wheel. I braced myself for the inevitability that we were about to be launched into the sky, but fortunately we came to another abrupt stop.

A small crowd had formed on the ground below The Big Thrill. They were talking and pointing up at us. Thank goodness! Hopefully someone would see that our cabins were breaking loose and they'd tell the operator so he could stop the ride. But then I heard an unexpected sound from the crowd. They were laughing at us! They thought we were just a bunch of kids panicking and overreacting.

They couldn't see Ghost Girl. They didn't know our lives were in actual danger either.

I was about to yell out for help when I spotted Beauregard. The real Beauregard, not Gary. He was standing in the centre of the crowd, staring up at us gleefully. The crowd must not have been able to see him, as one of them stepped right through the clown without any reaction at all.

"He's doing this!" I told Aaliyah, pointing at Beauregard. "He's going to kill us the same way he killed her." I indicated Ghost Girl.

"Don't say I didn't warn you," Ghost Girl said with an eerie lack of emotion.

Right on cue, our cabin flew backwards, stopped, then flew forward. That's when I noticed our cabin was on a track. As we descended, the track tilted up and down like a seesaw, sending us careening in one direction and then the other. The cabins above and below us were doing the same. Beauregard and Ghost Girl weren't controlling the cabin's movement . . . that's what it was supposed to do.

As I began to feel a little safer about the ride, anger replaced my fear.

"What do you want with us?" I yelled at Ghost Girl. "Does scaring people make you feel good?"

We slid back and forth again, and now that I knew to expect the movement, it didn't feel quite so jarring, nor did it sound like our cabin was about to break free.

"No," Ghost Girl said. "It doesn't make me feel good. Nothing makes me feel good. Nothing makes me *feel*, period."

"Then why are you trying to hurt us?" Aaliyah asked. "You're just like Beauregard."

Ghost Girl wrinkled her nose and pulled back her lips — I didn't think ghosts could throw up, but it looked like she was about to. "We're nothing like him. It's his fault we're dead, his fault we can't move on, his fault we're stuck here forever. And he's going to do the same to you."

Ghost Girl wasn't trying to hurt us, or even scare us. She was just a ghost with a grudge.

I scanned the crowd and was relieved to see that Beauregard had disappeared.

"If we help you move on," I said as an idea began to take

shape in my head, "would you help us get rid of Beauregard?"

"Yes, of course," Ghost Girl said with an enthusiastic nod. "But neither of those things are possible."

"I think they are," I said. "In fact, I think they're connected — we can make both happen at the same time."

Before I could explain any further, we reached the loading platform and the ride came to a stop. Harriett was there to greet us with a wide grin. Ghost Girl was consumed by mist and vanished before the attendant opened our cabin door and let us out. Sai and Jason also exited their cabin and looked shaky on their feet, like they might fall over with any step.

"How thrilling was that?" Harriett asked us eagerly. "I thought you were literally scared for your lives!"

"Well, we didn't know the cabin was going to slide back and forth," I said. "So yeah, that was pretty scary." It wasn't the only reason I'd been terrified, but I figured it would be best to leave it at that.

A smile lit up Harriett's face. "Isn't it an awesome addition to have the cabins slide back on forth on the descent?"

"It was awesome when I realized they were supposed to do that," I said. "Thanks a lot," I added.

"You're welcome, but I can't take all the credit," Harriett said, completely missing my sarcasm. "Beth and everyone else before me started the work, but I can tell the enhancements are going to be a big hit. The looks on your faces were priceless!" She laughed her way through the tail end of her sentence, barely finishing before she needed to take a deep breath. Once she'd resupplied her oxygen levels, she started laughing even harder.

"Right," I said, the word drawn out. I gently held Aaliyah's arm and waved at Sai and Jason to follow us, then began walking away. "We're going to go grab something to eat. I'm dying for a funnel cake."

Harriett was still so pleased by how the ride had performed and our reactions to it that she barely seemed to register what I'd said.

I wasn't dying for a funnel cake, of course. I was dying to share the plan that was forming in my head.

CHAPTER
Seventeen

Sai's hands were shaking and Jason's face was pale.

"That was pretty terrible," Jason said, hooking a thumb over his shoulder at The Big Thrill. "I feel ill."

"It certainly didn't improve my fear of heights," Sai said.

"But at least Ghost Girl returned," Jason said. "If not for that, it would have been a truly awful experience."

"What are you talking about?" Sai protested. "Ghost Girl *added* to the awfulness of the experience!"

"To each their own," Jason said. "What did she want?"

"Our conversation was brief, thankfully," I said. "But she did confirm that Beauregard tampered with The Big Thrill, which caused the accident that killed them. Did you see him?"

"He was in your cabin too?" Jason asked with a whine.

I shook my head. "I spotted him on the ground in the middle of the crowd. He was just staring up at us with this hideously happy expression, and then he disappeared."

"That clown's got issues," Sai said.

"Ghost Girl and her boyfriend, Nicholas, were the young couple we read about in that newspaper article Harriett gave me," Aaliyah said.

"Nicholas? You didn't happen to catch her name?" Jason asked sarcastically.

"No, but we now know why they're trapped here," I said. "They died too young, too tragically. But if we can help each other force Beauregard to move on . . ."

"They might be able to move on too," Jason finished.

"It's worth a shot, right?" I said.

"Wait, wait, wait," Sai said. "Are you saying what I think you're saying?"

We didn't say anything.

"That we're going to find Beauregard on purpose?" Sai said.

We still didn't say anything.

"And what?" Sai said. "Team up with a couple other ghosts in order to send the clown to that Neverwhere place?"

"The Netherrealm," Jason said, then he smiled. "It feels nice correcting you for a change."

"It's our best shot at protecting ourselves," I told Sai, "and the thousands of kids who are about to descend on Pennyland once it opens to the public."

He looked at each of us in turn and nodded. "All right.

I trust you. Whatever it is you're thinking of doing, I'm in."

He put his hand out, palm down.

I didn't want to leave him hanging. I quickly placed my hand on his.

Jason followed suit, as did Aaliyah.

"We're like the three musketeers," Aaliyah said, "only there are four of us."

"There actually were four musketeers," I said, "once D'Artagnan joined Athos, Aramis and Porthos."

Aaliyah, Jason and Sai all looked at me with various amounts of surprise and confusion.

I laughed. "Last year I signed on to star in an all-female retelling of *The Three Musketeers*, so I read the book, but the film fell apart during pre-production. It would've been my first feature film."

"Well, forget them — you've got us," Aaliyah said.

I smiled. "All for one and one for all!"

We raised our hands in the air.

"So, what's the plan?" Sai asked.

"We're going to watch Beauregard's show," Aaliyah said. "His *final* show."

I nodded. "But we're going to have the last laugh."

Aaliyah whistled appreciatively. "That was, like, a *Screamers*-worthy line."

"Thank you," I said with a grin.

Jason pumped his fist in the air. "Looks like we're going on a ghost hunt tonight! I'll go get my gear!"

"Don't forget the cheese puffs!" I reminded him.

Less than fifteen minutes later we met up in front of the circus tent. The rides were no longer running and the extras were beginning to file out of the park. The film crew were packing up their gear and the Pennyland staff were closing things up for the night.

Each of us had told our parents we were going to rehearse one of the next day's big scenes — to be filmed in the tent — which was the perfect cover. Hopefully it would be our last lie.

Although I knew we were doing what needed to be done, I wanted to be anywhere else.

ZOË WINTER RESISTS URGE TO RUN HOME TO HER MOMMY AND HIDE UNDER HER BED

The headline in my mind forced me to confront how I was feeling. I was scared, but accepting that gave me the power to do something about it. I took a deep breath and told myself I could do this. After all, it wasn't like I was alone. I was with friends.

"So, how do we summon Ghost Girl and her boyfriend?"

Sai asked. "You got any gear that can be used to call them?"

Jason shook his backpack up and down and shrugged. "I left my Ouija board at home. Too bulky."

"We don't need a Ouija board," I said, reaching into the bushes beside the entrance to the tent. I pulled out the cut-out of the one and only Beauregard.

HE LAUGHS! HE CRIES! HE'S A RIOT!

Somewhere in the distance I heard Beauregard's laughter. I spun around and looked behind me, then left, then in front, then right, but couldn't spot the clown. Then I looked behind me once more and dropped the cut-out.

Ghost Girl and Nicholas were standing in a whorl of mist.

"What have you done . . . *again?*" Ghost Girl said, staring at me intently.

"I've brought you here—" I said.

"What you've done will bring him here too," Ghost Girl said before I could elaborate. "He's connected to that sign somehow, and he knows whenever anyone touches it. And just like the last time, he's going to come for you."

"Good," I said, trying to sound brave. "That's what we want. I think we can make him move on, which will allow you to move on too."

Nicholas looked from me to his dead girlfriend. "Is that possible?" he asked desperately.

"I think so," I said. "We need to send Beauregard to the Netherrealm, and you're stuck here because of what he did to you. If you help us stop Beauregard, I believe you'll be free."

"Beauregard will never go to the Netherrealm willingly," Ghost Girl said. "He wants only one thing: To keep performing. To keep killing."

"Well, we're not going to ask him, pretty please with sugar on top, to leave this plane," Jason said.

"We're going to make him leave," Aaliyah added.

Ghost Girl and Nicholas looked at each of us in turn, their disbelieving stares settling on Sai.

He raised his hands and said, "Hey, don't look at me. This wasn't my plan. I just want to act, but here I am."

"He's powerful — much more powerful than us," Ghost Girl said. "Years ago we saw Beauregard open a passage to the Netherrealm."

"Where was the passage?" Jason asked.

Ghost Girl pointed at the tent. "There's a clown's face painted on the floor in the centre of the ring. It's where he hit the ground and died all those years ago. That night a hole opened in that very spot and the sounds of the dead poured out of it. We saw Beauregard staring into its depths. When he saw us watching him, he flew into a rage, the hole sealed up, and he chased us out of the tent with an evil cackle."

"That's it," I said to the others. "That's what we have to do."

"What, Zoë?" Aaliyah asked.

"We have to trick Beauregard into opening that passage again, and then we have to shove him down it."

"It won't work," Nicholas said. "He won't let you get close enough, and even if he did, it would be too dangerous."

"But not for us," Ghost Girl said. "Once we've had our revenge on Beauregard, we'll finally be free to pass on."

I nodded. "But until that time he can't have any suspicion that we're working together."

"All this sounds like great fun," Sai said sarcastically, "but how, exactly, are we supposed to trick him into doing what we want?"

"Leave that to me," I said. "I'm going to speak with him, performer to performer."

As I stepped through the entrance of the circus tent, it felt like there was an invisible barrier, some sort of force field, trying to keep me out. Or was it trying to keep something in? I shook my head and pushed on, begging my imagination to stop running away from reason and logic. There was no force field.

And if there's anything hiding in this tent, my imagination gleefully pointed out, *it wants you to come in.*

Jason, Aaliyah and Sai followed me. Ghost Girl and Nicholas remained hidden outside so Beauregard wouldn't know they were helping us. Rows of wooden benches surrounded the centre ring. Yellow stars covered the floor. A giant clown face was painted in the middle, just like the ghosts had said. A tightrope was stretched taut between two poles above the clown's head.

Sai scanned the length of the tightrope and then bent over and rested his hands on his knees. "Have I told you all how much I hate heights?"

"Repeatedly," Aaliyah said.

"Is that," Jason asked in disbelief, "an actual cannon?"

It was. Or at least it appeared to be, painted with red-and-white stripes.

Aaliyah walked to a small platform near the centre of the ring. There was a lion tamer's whip on it, which she picked up. She shuddered and dropped the whip.

"What is it?" I asked.

"Nothing," she said with a shiver. "I just . . . don't like this place. It gives me a bad vibe."

Although I didn't say it, I knew what she meant. My stomach had clenched and I felt a little dizzy. The bad feeling was back, but by now I'd learned to live with it. "It's probably the air in here," I said, trying to reassure the others. "It smells nasty, like old mushrooms."

"It reminds me of an athletic bag filled with old, sweaty hockey gear," Sai said. "I think we can all agree that the sooner we get this show on the road, the better. So how do we get the clown to appear?"

"Um, I think he's already here," Jason said. He was staring intently at his black-and-orange EMF sensor. He waved me over and tapped the screen. The number 65 appeared on the digital display. "Anything zero to ten is a low anomaly in the surrounding electromagnetic fields. Eleven to one hundred is medium. More than one hundred is high, and a beeper will sound. If you hear that—"

The number jumped to 101 and the sensor started beeping.

"That was fast," Jason said in quiet awe.

102, 103, 104 . . . The numbers climbed at a steady rate. 105, 120, 125, 130, 135, finally coming to a stop at 137.

Every muscle in my body tensed up, but what was I scared of? I already knew the tent was haunted and I wanted Beauregard to appear. But that didn't make things any less scary. *It's okay to be scared,* I told myself. *Just don't let it consume you.*

"Oh no!" Jason shouted suddenly.

"What?" I asked in a panic. "Is one thirty-seven bad?"

"No, I just realized I forgot the cheese puffs back in my trailer."

I sighed in relief, but Aaliyah didn't look comforted.

"Zoë, maybe this was a bad idea," she said.

"For the record, I'm with Aaliyah," Sai said.

I took a deep breath and spoke as calmly as possible. "There's no reason to panic. It's not like Beauregard is . . ."

I trailed off when I noticed Jason's terrified expression. He was staring behind me, slowly shaking his head.

"Jason?" I said, hating the pathetic tone in my voice.

He pointed a trembling finger over my shoulder, confirming what I had feared. "He's right behind you."

CHAPTER
Eighteen

I turned around slowly. Beauregard was standing in the centre of the tent, about five metres away. He stood as still as a statue, smiling like a hyena who'd just stumbled upon a leftover carcass.

I swallowed and steeled my nerve. "Beauregard," I said.

"Zoë," he replied.

"You know my name."

"Of course I do," he said. "Last night's little soiree in my funhouse wasn't the only time we've spent together. I've been watching you all, my excitement for this moment growing and growing. I can't wait to make you laugh and cry . . . and then die."

"We came here willingly," I said. "You're a performer, like me, so I understand you. You want to put on a show, and to do that you need an audience. We just want this to be over, so we'll watch your show and we won't bother you any-more if you let us go. That way we all get what we want."

Beauregard paused, tilted his head, and seemed to give it some thought. "You're willing to be my audience voluntarily?"

I almost laughed, partly in shock and partly in relief. I didn't think that would work. "Yes! Of course we are."

Beauregard started to laugh, low and slow at first, then louder and faster. He wiped away a tear and said, "Hoo boy. You should've seen the look on your face!" He mimicked me by widening his eyes and plastering a hopeful smile across his face, then laughed some more, this time slapping his knee and wiping away imaginary tears. "My dear girl, let me tell you something: I admire your naive optimism. I really do. It's going to make your deaths all the sweeter." He smiled so impossibly wide that his mouth was nearly as large as the entire lower half of his face, just like he'd done before attacking Aaliyah and me in The Laffin' Place, and I knew we were in trouble.

But before I could do anything, Beauregard raised his right hand and snapped his fingers. With a crack of electricity, every light turned off and the tent was plunged into absolute darkness. I stood helplessly still as I listened to the sounds around me. Beauregard's laughter floated from left to right and front to back. There was a flickering of light as one after the other I heard Aaliyah, Sai and Jason scream, yell and grunt in pain. Then, from somewhere in the darkness, Beauregard grabbed my arms, twisted them behind my back, and shoved me hard, forcing me forward. The lights flickered again and I felt something hot surrounding my wrists. I tried to pull my arms apart but my wrists were bound together. Beauregard shoved me down by the shoulders and I landed hard on something solid.

I heard another finger snap and the lights turned back on. I was sitting on one of the front-row benches with my friends beside me. Their hands were held behind their backs too, bound with a thin wisp of what looked like bluish-white electricity.

Beauregard stood before us with a maniacal smile, but he also looked a little tired, like his actions had drained him of energy. He took a deep breath and raised his hands. The lights flickered and, amazingly, four small streaks like tiny lightning bolts flew straight for us. In the flash of an eye our ankles were bound by thin streaks of blue light, just like our wrists. Although Beauregard now looked completely exhausted and powerless, we were trapped.

"Electric bonds?" Sai said. "Why couldn't he have used — oh, I don't know — thin balloon strings to restrain us?"

"I knew ghosts could control electricity to some degree," Jason said, looking at his ankles in awe, "but this is next-level stuff."

"I'm glad one of us is enjoying this," Aaliyah said.

"Don't worry," I told them quietly. "The plan will still work." But would it? I was beginning to have some serious doubts. Ghost Girl and Nicholas had told us Beauregard was powerful, and the fact that he could somehow channel electricity to bind us was further proof of that. At least using that power seemed to slow him down temporarily, but not long enough for my liking. He stood up straight and spread his arms wide.

"Ladies and gentlemen, boys and girls, children of all ages," he said, spinning around on the spot and addressing the nearly empty tent. He faced us again and settled his gaze upon us. No longer laughing or smiling, Beauregard looked downright angry. "It's time to start the show."

I struggled and thrashed and tried to pull my legs and arms apart, but the electric bonds didn't even budge. There was nothing I could do.

But then I had an idea. "The last time you performed each of the circus roles, more than eighty years ago, it killed you. You're no lion tamer or trapeze artist. You're just a stupid clown. And nobody likes clowns."

Beauregard's lips curled into a sneer and his eyes narrowed. I heard something faint, like a low growl, rumbling in the back of his throat.

"Zoë?" Aaliyah hissed in desperation. "What are you doing?"

I ignored her and plowed on, hoping this desperate move would work. "But all four of us — not just me — we're all performers too. If you free us, together we can all put on a bigger and better show than you could do on your own."

Beauregard roared so loud that the circus lights flickered rapidly and shut off. When they turned back on a moment later, Beauregard was standing right in front of me. He craned his head down, his eyes wild and his lips stretched across his face, coming to a narrow stop mere centimetres from my nose. His teeth were close enough to tear a chunk out of my face.

"You want to be in my show?" he said.

"Yes," I said, too afraid to nod with our heads so close together.

Beauregard laughed. "Now that you mention it, this could be a lot of fun." He looked from me to Aaliyah, Jason and Sai, and then he smiled. "Places, everyone. The show's about to begin!"

All of a sudden I got to my feet, but I wasn't in control. It felt like I was a puppet on strings. Beauregard was controlling me and the others with the electric bonds. He turned and walked back to centre stage. The four of us were pulled behind him as if on leashes. We came to an abrupt stop and the clown walked around us in a tight circle.

My friends split up and started walking in three different directions. Beauregard left me standing where I was as doubt began to weigh me down. I had hoped he might free our arms and legs, but he was obviously too clever for that. Had I overreached? Had I pushed Beauregard too far? Would he take the final piece of bait I had yet to dangle in front of him? Would Ghost Girl and Nicholas come through? My concerns were stacking up but it was too late to turn back now.

The other three reached the destinations Beauregard had intended for them.

Jason slipped into the cannon. "Zoë?" he said helplessly before disappearing from view.

Sai whimpered as he climbed a ladder to the acrobat's platform three or four storeys in the air.

Aaliyah stepped up onto the lion tamer's platform and picked up the whip. She looked around nervously, no doubt terrified that Beauregard had a lion hidden somewhere backstage. Why else would he have led her there?

Beauregard raised his hands in the air and sparks of electricity zigzagged between his fingers. He looked at me with fire in his eyes and said, "You might want to take half a step back."

I was forced backwards just as a hole a metre in diameter opened where I had stood a heartbeat before. A full-grown lion leapt out of the floor, and the hole sealed again, causing Beauregard to laugh and whoop in approval. The animal had a faint blue glow radiating off its fur and it roared loud enough for me to feel reverberations in my eardrums. Ghost or not — the lion was dangerous, that much was clear. It sniffed derisively at me and I felt my insides turn to jelly, and then it paced in circles around Aaliyah. She began to cry silently.

"You must be wondering what part you get to play in tonight's extra-special show," Beauregard said. He sounded tired and out of breath, likely from opening the portal to the Netherrealm and summoning the lion. "You get the night off, Zoë — you've earned it. You get to stand here next to me and watch your friends die."

CHAPTER
Nineteen

I looked from the lion to the cannon to Sai standing on the thin platform high in the air, and I swallowed hard. I had to keep my nerve. I had to carry on — there was no turning back now.

I cleared my throat and forced the words out. "One person doesn't make an audience."

Beauregard looked from the lion to me, his smile faltering. "What was that?"

"I said, one person doesn't make an audience. I've read about you and your early days at Pennyland. You used to fill this tent every night, seven days a week. People loved your show. But now?" I shrugged and looked around the tent, waving my bound hands at the stands to reinforce their emptiness. "No one cares. People hate clowns these days. The world has moved on. You're just too stubborn — or stupid — to accept that."

Beauregard grabbed my wrist and squeezed. Electricity

crackled through his hair as he snarled and looked at me with pure fury. My arm felt like it had been encased in ice. The cold sensation spread rapidly through my body and I struggled to breathe. With my hands and feet still bound, I couldn't fight back or run away. My heartbeat seemed to slow. My vision faded. I felt tired, like the life was being sucked out of my body and I was powerless to stop it.

I slumped forward in Beauregard's grasp, and he released me with a disgusted grunt. "As much joy and happiness as killing you will bring me, it's too soon. I don't want you to die before the fun begins. You're right that one person doesn't make an audience, and you're also right that people today wouldn't appreciate my show." He raised his balled fists to his eyes and pretended to cry with an exaggerated "boo-hoo," then smiled. "But people from my time would."

As tired and sore as I was, I felt a spark of hope ignite inside of me. Beauregard had taken the bait, but I was careful not to smile or do anything else that would betray how I felt — I couldn't let him know I'd planted the very seed in his mind that was now blooming.

He raised his hands in the air again and opened the portal to the Netherrealm once more.

After a moment or two I heard voices coming from below. A little boy emerged from the hole, flanked by two adults. They were dressed in old-fashioned clothing and the boy carried a cotton-candy cone. He smiled widely when he took in his surroundings.

"It's a circus show!" the boy said. "Thank you, Mommy! Thank you, Daddy!"

The boy and his parents were followed by a steady stream of ghosts from another time. Kids, teens, adults. They took their seats on the benches, filling the tent. Beauregard had his audience.

"Popcorn!" a man called out. He held a snack tray with straps over his shoulders. "Get your popcorn here! Fresh, hot popcorn!" A woman had a tray of drinks, and another man was selling circus-themed trinkets and toys from a small cart on wheels.

"What a sight," Beauregard told me quietly, appreciating the crowd he had summoned. He looked more tired than before. The portal to the Netherrealm slowly shrunk as I scanned the audience for Ghost Girl and Nicholas.

Come, on, come on, come on. Where are they? What are they waiting for?

It was the perfect time to drag Beauregard down, but as the hole closed so too did our window of opportunity.

Finally I spotted them as they floated through one of the tent's walls . . . but it was too late. The portal was shut.

No! My heart sank. That was our one and only chance to be rid of Beauregard before he killed us, and I didn't know how else to stop him.

All the lights shut off with a loud *crack*, except for one —
a spotlight aimed directly at Beauregard. "And here . . .
we . . . go," he whispered to me out of the side of his mouth.
Then he turned to the audience, spread his arms in a wel-
coming gesture, and smiled.

"Are you ready to be thrilled?" he asked loudly, taking
on the role of a circus ringmaster. "It's time for the acrobat
to fly through the air — watch out! There's no safety net."

Sai was forced to take a shaky step forward. The toes
of his shoes stuck out over the ledge of the platform. His
arms shot up and grabbed the trapeze.

"It's time for the human cannonball to be fired from the
cannon," Beauregard said. "You'll be amazed by how far he
flies!"

Jason's hands reached out of the cannon and waved to the
crowd, his electric band shaking his hands side to side.

"And last but not least," Beauregard said, "does our lion
tamer dare to face the beast? Beware the jaws. They bite!
And the claws. They catch!"

Aaliyah cracked the whip as the lion prowled around her
platform. The animal roared and the crowd went wild.

"It's showtime!" Beauregard called.

Sai took a step off the platform, the wick on the rear end
of the cannon ignited, and the lion raised one of its large
paws to take a swipe at Aaliyah.

"Wait!" I shouted.

Beauregard raised a hand, and everything froze — Sai, the burning wick, the lion and even the entire audience. The clown was in complete control.

"What is it, Zoë?" Beauregard asked. "This had better be good."

I had no idea what to say, but I knew I had to stop him before my friends died. "If you kill me and my friends, we'll stay here to haunt you forever. We'll find a way to make you move on. We'll force you to the Netherrealm."

Beauregard howled and the audience unfroze for a moment to join in the chorus of laughter. "My, my, my. You do have quite the imagination, don't you, Zoë? You think you four will be able to stop me after you die?

"I don't think you're as strong as you say you are," I said, my mind racing. I didn't have a clear plan and was making things up as I went. And then, thankfully, I had a thought. "Every time you've controlled electricity or opened the Netherrealm portal, it's exhausted you. You don't have enough strength left to open it again. We'll escape. We'll figure out how to open the portal ourselves . . ." I had saved my finishing blow for this moment. "Lon Beaumont."

"SILENCE!" Beauregard bellowed. He bared his teeth and knocked me to the ground. Beauregard stood above me and pinned me down with one of his oversized shoes. "That name is dead to me. That man is dead to me. I am the one and only Beauregard!"

It worked. Jason had said ghosts' names held a little power over them, and Beauregard's name had the power to enrage him . . . and hopefully make him act foolishly.

Beauregard knelt down and put his hand on my back. Suddenly it was as though the air was being squeezed from my lungs, making it impossible to take a breath. It felt like my ribs might break at any moment. Something about his touch seemed to suck the life right out of my body. I'd felt this once before, when Ghost Girl had grabbed my throat in The Laffin' Place. Stars danced in my eyes and the world spun around me. Beauregard reached for my head and turned it to the side.

"NEVER QUESTION MY POWER!" he roared as he reached his free hand toward the middle of the circus stage.

I couldn't breathe, my back ached, my torso felt like it was on fire and my vision was narrowing to a tiny circle of light.

Sparks danced between Beauregard's fingertips, and the hole in the ground opened once more, this time more slowly than before. But this time I knew it was for me.

The last thing I saw was Nicholas and Ghost Girl streaming toward us in a rush of mist. He tackled the clown and dragged him toward the portal, but she came for me. I couldn't think why she wasn't helping her boyfriend take down Beauregard — I literally didn't have enough brainpower left. My final thought was a simple hope that

Aaliyah, Sai and Jason — three of the four musketeers — would somehow survive. Otherwise my death would be meaningless.

I took my final breath. My heart took its final beat. I closed my eyes and died.

CHAPTER
Twenty

Blackness—

Nothingness—

Floating in an empty void—

And then—

My body felt like it had been given a jump start by car booster cables. I rocketed up into a seated position and sucked in a large gasp of breath. Ghost Girl was crouched in front of me, a mixture of nerves and relief on her face. She looked down at my chest and I followed her gaze. Her hand was inside me. I felt the oddest ticklish sensation on my heart as she withdrew her hand.

"Your heart stopped," she said. "I started it again."

"Thank you," I said, rubbing my sore back. "You saved my life, so I guess I can't be too mad that you and Nicholas were a little late."

"Sorry about that," Ghost Girl said. "We panicked a little and hesitated outside the tent."

I almost patted her on the back before remembering she was a ghost and that my hand, now free of its electric bonds, would pass straight through her. "I get it, and I was just teasing. You got here just in time, and that's what counts."

"Help!" Nicholas shouted from a few metres away. Although Beauregard was nearly drained from the exertion of opening the portal to the Netherrealm three times in a short period of time, the clown was still putting up a desperate fight.

I tried to get to my feet but Ghost Girl held up her hand to stop me. "It has to be us. We have to force him through the portal or we'll never be free." She stood up to help her boyfriend.

"Wait," I said. Before she left, there was something I needed to know. "What's your name? There's power in names, and I want to make sure I remember you by yours."

A smile flickered across her face. "It's Florence." She flew the short distance from me to Nicholas and wrapped her arms around Beauregard. The clown wasn't able to overpower both Florence and Nicholas at the same time, and the three of them tipped over the ledge and tumbled into the chasm.

The last thing I saw before they disappeared was the fear that filled Beauregard's face. He was no longer laughing, nor crying — the only emotion on his face was terror.

The electric bonds around my ankles and wrists fizzled out and I was able to move freely again. Aaliyah leapt off the pedestal, away from the lion, just as the beast unfroze and took a swipe through the air where she'd previously stood. She ran to my side. Instead of following her, the lion bounded toward the portal and jumped into it. The hole was slowly closing. The remaining ghosts — Beauregard's summoned audience — snapped out of their trance-like states too and, sensing they were about to be trapped on this plane with no way of returning to the Netherrealm, rushed to follow the lion. Together they poured into the portal like a waterfall of light, and before long they had all returned from where they had come. The portal sealed itself a moment after the last ghost flew through it.

The silence that followed was eerie.

Jason pulled himself out of the cannon and stood up a little shakily.

Sai called down from the raised platform. "One last time: I *hate* heights."

Aaliyah and Jason helped him down and the three of them joined me at the centre of the ring.

"I can't believe you did it!" Aaliyah said, wrapping her arms around me in a tight embrace. "I mean, I never doubted you."

"You don't need to lie," I said with a laugh. "I had my doubts too. And if it weren't for Florence and Nicholas, we wouldn't have." It felt good using her name, and I was happy she had entrusted me with it. It felt even better hugging Aaliyah, knowing that after all we'd been through we'd be friends forever, no matter where life took us.

"You were incredible," Sai said. "Maybe your best performance ever, and that's saying something."

"Thanks, Sai," I said. "Coming from such a talented actor as you, that means a lot to me."

"What happened?" Jason asked. He hadn't seen a thing from inside the cannon.

"So you're telling me," he said in frustration after we'd filled him in, "that a hundred or so old-timey spectres and a phantom lion were summoned into this tent before a couple of vengeful spirits dragged an evil ghost clown through an interdimensional portal to the Netherrealm, and the one person here who is obsessed with the paranormal *missed* it?"

"In a nutshell, yes," Sai said.

"I hate you all," Jason said with remarkable good humour, given the circumstances. His stomach growled and he placed a hand on his belly. "Anyone else starving?"

"How can you think of food right now?" Aaliyah said.

Jason shrugged and said, "Ghost hunting always works up an appetite. Zoë gets it."

I nodded. "I could really go for a bag of cheese puffs. Family size."

"See?" Jason said. His eyes widened and he pointed at a tray of snacks scattered on the ground near the front row of benches. "Is that what I think it is?"

"It's popcorn," I confirmed. Apparently the vendor had dropped the tray in his haste to return to the Netherrealm and the snacks had remained here.

Jason took a step toward the food, but Sai grabbed his arm and stopped him. "Dude, that's *ghost* popcorn."

Jason broke free, scooped up a couple of half-filled bags, and returned to us. "Don't worry. I'll share."

"You gotta be kidding me," Sai said.

"No way am I going to put that into my body," Aaliyah said.

Jason held one of the bags out to me and smiled encouragingly.

"Thanks, but I'll pass," I said, trying to sound polite.

"Suit yourself," Jason said, emptying the popcorn from one of the bags into the other. "More for the rest of us — well, more for me."

"Are you actually going to eat that?" Sai asked. "You don't know what it will do to you."

In answer, Jason took a handful of popcorn and shoved it in his mouth. He smiled as he chewed, but then his smile froze. His eyes went wide. He looked sick and panicked. He started to make loud gagging sounds and put his hand to his throat.

"Jason!" Sai shouted.

Jason dropped the act and laughed, spewing a mouthful of partially chewed popcorn all over the ground in front of him.

"You jerk!" Sai shouted.

"C'mon, it was funny," Jason said. He offered me the bag of popcorn. "You have to try this. It's absolutely delicious."

I accepted the bag and felt my hunger pangs immediately intensify. I picked up one piece of popcorn, studied it closely, sniffed it, licked it, and then finally put it in my mouth and chewed. I sighed.

"What is it?" Aaliyah asked, a slight note of concern in her voice.

"It's really good."

"See?" Jason said with a triumphant smile. "Getting to try ghost popcorn almost makes up for everything I missed out on while I was stuck in that stupid cannon. My friends back home are going to be seriously impressed."

I passed the bag to Aaliyah and Sai, and seeing that neither Jason nor I had died or turned into ghosts ourselves, they each took a handful of popcorn. We sat on one of the benches and passed the bag back and forth until it was empty, none of us particularly eager to part ways for the night.

Sitting safe and sound, shoulder to shoulder with my friends, was exactly where I wanted to be.

CHAPTER
Twenty-One

"**A**nd that's a wrap on Zoë Winter!" Clarice said.

I'd just finished filming my last scene of "The Scream Queen," and the set erupted in applause. Although nearly five days had passed since we sent Beauregard to the Netherrealm, I still thought of the clown and circus tent every time I heard clapping.

I smiled and nodded appreciatively at the cast and crew surrounding me. "Thanks, everyone. This has been a very . . . interesting shoot. I'm proud of the work we've all done and can't wait to see the finished show. I don't want to jinx anything, but I think this is going to be the best, most talked about episode of *Screamers* ever!"

More applause, the loudest of all coming from my three friends. Hugs and high-fives were shared all around.

"Great work, Zoë," Clarice said, joining the four of us. "You really dug deep and tapped into some powerful emotions for this episode. Things started a little shaky that first day or two, but then at times I forgot you were acting and thought you were genuinely afraid for your life."

"This creepy set helped me get into character," I said. Clarice would never know the full truth of that statement.

"Hey, that's my park you're calling creepy," Harriett said, appearing suddenly behind us.

"Oh, sorry," I said in embarrassment. "I didn't mean to insult you or Pennyland or—"

Harriett raised her hands and shook her head. "Zoë, Zoë, Zoë. It's okay! I was only joking. This isn't *my* park — I only work here. Plus, you're right — it's totally creepy!"

I sighed in relief and noticed that Harriett's uniform finally had her own name on it. I pointed to the badge and said, "Beth's a thing of the past?"

"I guess the owners like me enough to have splurged for my own name badge," she said. "I think I've now worked here longer than most of the previous lead technicians. Take that, curse!"

"Good for you, Beth," Jason said.

Sai punched Jason's arm and said, "Dude! Zoë just said her name, plus it's literally on her uniform now."

"It's been a long week," Jason offered weakly.

"I've been meaning to tell you," Clarice said. "I had a talk with Pennyland's owners this morning and they'd like to invite the four of you back here for the park's grand re-opening!"

"I'm in!" Jason said.

"Me too," Aaliyah said.

"Me three," Sai added.

"That makes four of us," I said, already beginning to mentally pack my bags. I'd been a little down thinking about us all returning to our hometowns the following day, so the thought of a reunion instantly cheered me up.

"I can see the headline now," Clarice said. "Scream Queen Zoë Winter Makes Triumphant Return to Famous *Screamers* Set."

I laughed but saw a different headline in my mind.

SCREAM QUEEN ZOË WINTER FINDS HAPPINESS HANGING OUT WITH NEW FRIENDS

It was probably the world's most boring headline in the history of boring headlines and it wouldn't entice a single person to read the rest of the article, but it was the only headline I wanted to see in my future. I smiled and laughed a little to myself.

Glenda approached with a man I hadn't seen in six months.

"Hi, Jeremy," I said.

"Hey, Zoë," Jeremy replied warmly. He was wearing a blazer and a *Ghostbusters* T-shirt, his signature look. "I hear this is going to be quite the memorable episode."

"Wait," Jason said. "Jeremy? As in Jeremy Alexander Sinclair?"

"Of course!" Glenda said. "Don't you remember I told you on our first night that he'd be visiting at the end of the shoot?"

"It's been a long week," Clarice told Glenda, echoing what Jason had said a little earlier.

"Pleased to meet you all," Jeremy said. He shook hands with everyone. "You must be Jason, right?"

Jason's face went beet red. "Jeremy Alexander Sinclair knows my name," he said in awe.

"Jeremy Sinclair is fine, or just Jeremy. Only my book covers call me by my middle name."

"Book covers," Sai said with a snap of his fingers. "You're the author of Screamers."

"Guilty as charged," Jeremy said.

"You're just realizing that now?" Aaliyah teased Sai. "Try to keep up!"

Sai shrugged and said, "It's been a—"

"Long week!" Clarice, Glenda and I all finished.

"He also writes Haunted Coasts, the series of true ghost stories," Jason said. "I wish I had my copies with me so you could sign them. I have every single book you've ever written."

"Jason is not only an actor, but also a ghost hunter," Aaliyah added. "And a really good one too. He has, like, gear and stuff. With buttons and screens and detectors. And he taught us all about the importance of cheese puffs."

"Wise man," Jeremy said. "One should never underestimate the value of proper snacking during a ghost hunt. But I'm more of a popcorn person myself."

The other kids and I shared a laugh at that. The grown-ups couldn't have known the true reason we'd found Jeremy's quip so funny.

"Anyway, don't worry," Jeremy told Jason. "I'll be happy to send you a signed advance copy of my latest novel. It's about a haunted corn maze and, well, spoiler alert: things don't go well for the characters."

Jason opened his mouth to speak but no words came out. For the first time since I'd met him, he was speechless. He closed his mouth and nodded, looking a little like he might cry.

"Sorry, everyone," Glenda said, "but Mr. Sinclair is in the middle of a book tour and his next flight is at fifteen hundred, so we need to go."

Sai looked at me and cocked an eyebrow. "Five o'clock?"

I shook my head. "Three o'clock," I corrected. As smart as Sai was, I'd been trying to teach him military time all week and it had not gone well.

"Well, it was a pleasure meeting you three," Jeremy told Jason, Sai and Aaliyah. "And always a pleasure seeing you,

Zoë. I'm sorry I couldn't stay longer but I'm glad I got to stop by the set to say keep up the great work."

A photographer took a few promotional shots of the four of us with Jeremy and then Glenda led him away, checking her phone to make sure the details of his trip were all lined up.

"I need to sit down," Jason said. He looked around for a chair but, finding none, opted to sit cross-legged on the ground. He looked like he'd died and gone to heaven.

"So, Zoë," Clarice said, "what's next for you? Other than season three of *Screamers*, any work lined up?"

"Not yet," I said, my curiosity piqued as I noticed that Clarice was hiding something behind her back. "What have you got there?"

"A script," she said, revealing a bound stack of paper.

"The next episode?"

She shook her head. "A feature film I've written. An adaptation, actually."

"Of a book?"

"No, not a book. A video game you might have heard of." She held the script up so I could read the title.

KILL SCREEN:
GHOSTS NEVER DIE

"What's a kill screen?" I asked.

"What's a kill screen?" Sai asked me incredulously.

"Zoë, *Kill Screen* is only, like, the hottest game on the planet right now," Aaliyah said, speaking slowly as if I were half her age, or had half her brain mass. "You've seriously never heard of it?"

I shrugged. "I've been busy." *Plus,* I thought, *I don't have many friends my own age.*

Correction: I didn't *have many friends my own age . . . before now.*

"How about you guys teach me how to play?" I said. "We can stay up all night until we beat it."

Jason laughed from his seat on the floor. "Good luck. The game's unbeatable."

"No game is unbeatable," I said with a laugh, but no one laughed with me. "Right?"

"This one is," Sai added. "Trust me, I've spent hours trying."

"So if the game's unbeatable, how is the movie going to end?" I asked Clarice.

"You've got to read the script to find out," she said, handing it to me. "I want you to play the lead."

It felt heavier in my hands than it should have, as if it was somehow weighing me down to the point I couldn't move. My first instinct was to flip through the pages to see how meaty the role was. But I hesitated, the script continuing to paralyze me.

And then I did something that surprised me. I handed the script back to Clarice.

"You don't . . . want to read it?" she asked, looking from me to the script and back to me again.

"No offence, Clarice — I'm sure the script is great and it might seem foolish of me to turn down the lead role . . ." I swallowed, ran a hand through my hair, and took a deep breath, my mind racing. Was I doing the right thing? Was I making a mistake? Would I regret this later? I shook my head and plowed on. "But I don't want to overcommit to anything right now. I want some free time to just . . . be me." *Nice, down to earth, a normal kid.*

Suddenly I felt a hundred times lighter, and I knew I'd made the right choice.

Clarice smiled and nodded. "Okay. I get that. Maybe, if it's a big hit, I can talk you into signing on for the sequel."

I shrugged and returned her smile, relieved she wasn't upset by my decision. "Who knows? Maybe. But for now, since you asked what's next for me, I'm thinking I'd like to go on vacation before school and filming start up again."

"Asia?" Aaliyah asked.

"Europe?" Sai asked.

"A road trip to visit the most-haunted locations in the country?" Jason asked.

"Jason's the closest," I said. "I'd like to visit each of you in your hometowns, if that's cool with you."

Jason stood up quickly and shared looks with Sai and Aaliyah. They all nodded and agreed enthusiastically.

"Great!" I said. "Let's take a pic together to celebrate the end of filming."

Aaliyah handed Clarice her phone and we draped our arms over each other's shoulders for the picture. Clarice took a few and handed the phone back. Aaliyah slipped it into her pocket.

"Oh, go on," I told her. "Posting one pic of us to Instagram won't hurt anything."

Aaliyah smiled and took her phone back out. "Well, okay. One post."

As she typed on her phone and the boys began talking about how excited they were to stay up all night playing video games, my mind wandered back to *Kill Screen*. *A game with no way to beat it. No ending.* That was an appealing thought. The future was unwritten. There was no way to know what was in store for any of us. Even better, you could write your own ending, and if I ever decided I wanted to change gears and take a permanent break from acting, well, that choice was mine to make. But I was sure that wherever my future was headed, I was going there with my new friends.

"Just tell me one thing before we start playing *Kill Screen*," I said as we started to leave Pennyland. "There aren't any clowns in this game, right?"

Photo credit: Colleen Morris

Joel A. Sutherland is an author and librarian. He is the author of several books in the Haunted Canada series, as well as *Be a Writing Superstar*, *Summer's End* and Haunted, a series of middle-grade horror novels. His short fiction has appeared in many anthologies and magazines, alongside the likes of Stephen King and Neil Gaiman. He has been a juror for the John Spray Mystery Award and the Monica Hughes Award for Science Fiction and Fantasy.

He appeared as "The Barbarian Librarian" on the Canadian edition of the hit television show Wipeout, making it all the way to the third round and proving that librarians can be just as tough and wild as any-one else.

Joel lives with his family in southeastern Ontario, where he is always on the lookout for ghosts.

ALSO AVAILABLE

HAUNTED
FIELD OF SCREAMS
JOEL A. SUTHERLAND

978-1-4431-6323-1

HAUNTED
NIGHT OF THE LIVING DOLLS
JOEL A. SUTHERLAND

978-1-4431-6325-5

HAUNTED
KILL SCREEN
JOEL A. SUTHERLAND

978-1-4431-5712-4

HAUNTED
THE HOUSE NEXT DOOR
JOEL A. SUTHERLAND

978-1-4431-5709-4